Brainard Allsworth

Tales and legends of two republics

Brainard Allsworth

Tales and legends of two republics

ISBN/EAN: 9783337174675

Printed in Europe, USA, Canada, Australia, Japan

Cover: Foto ©Andreas Hilbeck / pixelio.de

More available books at **www.hansebooks.com**

CUPID AND THE CANNON.

And written on the unhewed stone
That marks his grave, Unknown, Unknown. – p. 81.

TALES AND LEGENDS

OF

TWO REPUBLICS.

BY

B. W. ALLSWORTH.

Though lacking gold, we never stooped
  To pick it up in all our days;
Though lacking praise, we sometimes drooped,
  We never asked a soul for praise.
The exquisite reward of song
  Was song —the self-same thrill and glow
Which to unfolding flowers belong
  And wrens and thrushes know.
                        —T. B. ALDRICH.

TOPEKA, KANSAS:
HALL & O'DONALD LITHO. CO.
1889.

CONTENTS.

CONTENTS.

PREFACE.

This little volume is the *work* of no one. It is the *plaything* of one to whom an idle hour is very rare; and, in fact, it has been mostly written in moments stolen from sleep. The original intention was to treat largely of Mexico and South America, especially the former, both of which countries the writer has visited. Some personal knowledge of Mexico, and the ability to read and talk its language to a slight extent, together with the possession of a considerable number of MSS. left him by an educated Mexican, partly of the Aztec blood, led the writer to think of translations and legends.

Mexico is very rich in its legends and traditions. Too late, however, it became apparent that a lack of time utterly precluded the idea of having them ready as promised; hence the substitution of others. Of those given instead, some, at least, were written merely for self-gratification, and without any thought of them ever being published. He thought that those substituted were prepared with at least more care than the first mentioned, but latterly he has commenced to doubt even that; however, "What is writ is writ." A work for general circulation was not and is not contemplated. This is an age of books and book-making, and it is no longer held a crime to write one, and writing verses

is as innocent as the average amusement. It may
be that it contains imitations, but if so they were
not intended, and memory has been mistaken for
invention.

He wishes to say, as Touchstone did of his wife,
"If it's an ill-favored thing it's mine own." As to
measures and stanzas, no claim to originality is
made. Such as it is, it is given to those whom
personal acquaintance or curiosity may lead to ex-
amine it, with but little concern as to its fate; yet
the writer does not wish to be understood as being
indifferent to censure and praise.

> "Ere half the good I planned to do
> Was done, the short-breathed day was through.
> Had my intents been dark instead of fair
> I had done all, and still had time to spare."

TOPEKA, KANSAS, May, 1889.

CUM BONA VENIA.

The Muse, they say, is ever mute
  Upon the prairies bleak and wild,
And never wakes the lyre or lute
  For any save the mountain child:
That rugged hills and laughing rills
  Alone inspire the measured strain;
That harp strings break, and cannot wake
  An echo on the boundless plain;
    That all the notes are lost, the reed is tuned
      in vain.

No Delphi's fountain murmurs past:
  No fabled goddess wakes the strings:
No pean notes or stirring blast
  Inspires the soul, alone he sings.
In waking hours, in times of sleep—
  Perhaps it is delusion's snare —
Strange fancies o'er the mind will creep,
  And phantom voices fill the air;—
    Though rough may be the way, it lifts a
      weight of care.

Although his last faint notes may die
  Before to-morrow's dews shall fall,
And never from his hearthstone fly,

In vain, in vain it is not all.
It brings relief, a balm unknown
    To placid minds that never stray
Beyond the calm but frigid zone,
    Through which winds life's romanceless way.
    O wake, ye prairie winds, though rude may
        be your sway.

HOME AND MOTHER.

A child, upon the village street
    One morning idly straying,
Too far pursued with careless feet
    Her thoughtless round of playing;
She looked upon the passers-by,
    First one and then another;
Alarmed, the child commenced to cry.
    "I want my home and mother."

On battle field, a wounded boy,
    Where shots of death were screaming,
Forgot his sorrow, in the joy
    Of childhood sweetly dreaming.
As lower burned life's feeble spark,
    He whispered, "Sister, brother,
It grows so dark, so very dark,
    I'm going home to mother."

In far off city roamed a youth,
    Where crime's dark snare was reaching;
Of late far straying from the truth,
    And from his early teaching.
When asked to deeper drink the gall,
    He strove a sob to smother;
He answered this—and this was all—
    "I see my home and mother."

The wife that rocks and softly sings,
  Her prattling hope caressing,
Sees time recede on lightning wings,
  And deems this earth a blessing.
The husband sitting by her side,
  His love but growing stronger,
Smiles as he did upon his bride,
  And wishes life was longer.

The names the child first learns to speak,
  With lisping tongue uncertain;
And murmured last, in accents weak,
  As death rolls down the curtain.
Within this world no more to dwell,
  But leaving for another,
Be this to earth thy glad farewell,
  "I 'm going home to mother."

Domestic love, a wreath divine,
  A wreath all pure and holy:
Long may thy fadeless flowers entwine
  The cottage of the lowly.
Around the palace hearthstone bloom,
  Where dwell the noble hearted;
Thy power is vain to pierce the gloom,
  Where kindness has departed.

The patriot, doomed abroad to roam
  Where lordling rules his manor,
Sighs for his country and his home,
  Where floats our starry banner.

No other nation, like our own,
    Where king and serf are brother;
Where home is palace, court, and throne;
    An uncrowned queen, the mother.

THE TEACHER.

"How shall we add to earthly beauty?"
    An angel asked one day.
"By teaching man it is his duty
    To smooth his neighbor's way.

"To teach mankind the art of living,
    Is doing Heaven's will;
It would be well if more were giving
    To that their time and skill.

"'T is true, if judged by earthly measure,
    They toil for little pay;
And very few their hours of leisure,
    If faithful on the way.

"When conscious that they know their mission
    And do their labor right,
It gives to life a rich fruition,
    And makes the dark seem bright."

The angel smiled, and said with laughter,
    "I'm going with a crown."
A host of angels started after,
    And quickly followed down.

They placed the crown, with richest blessing,
  Upon the teacher's brow;
If she is onward, upward pressing,
  She wears it even now.

TO A YOUNG LADY.

When the summer roses fade,
  When the fairest lilies die,
I still see them, gentle maid,
  See their beauties in thy eye.

THE RUINS OF JAMESTOWN, VA.

The rank weed grows, the lizard crawls,
  The fate of all things telling;
The slimy serpent climbs the walls
  Of ancient church and dwelling;
The owl repeats her mournful calls,
Whose sound, like words of warning, falls,
  The timid step repelling.

Among the brambles growing 'round,
  There lie some silent sleepers;
'T is shameful to neglect the ground,
  The tombs entwined with creepers
Until the graves are scarcely found;
While all our states with wealth abound,
  They wait, the ruin keepers.

The first now gone, the last may fade,
   And when neglected lying
What now are busy marts of trade,
   Some traveler may be trying
To find the causes that have made
The ruins of Time's fatal blade,
   He sees around him dying.

It is not meet that man should mourn,
   His soul with sorrow burning;
We all must reach that silent bourn,
   But never one returning;
Be from our friends and kindred torn
In youth, or when with labor worn
   Some peaceful slumber earning.

Perchance the spirits in the sky,
   May, from their lofty station,
From out their starry realms on high,
   Gaze on earth's population;
With pleasure know that people sigh,
And deck the place *their* bodies lie,
   And smile *their* approbation.

THE GHOST.

The sable King of Night was on his throne,
   And quiet reigned until the hour of ten;
The bleak March winds began to sigh and
     moan;

And wilder gust I never faced, than when
The old town clock, from out its lofty tower,
Proclaimed, as with a prophet's warning power:
"Time rolls his ceaseless course!" It is the mid-
     night hour.

For wildest storm what need had I to care?
    A strapping youth with heart full light and
      gay,
Since I had been to see my lady fair,
    And she—ah well! had named the happy day.
At first, my path across the meadows led,
Then turned into a churchyard, where, 'tis said,
The spirits sometimes walk, the spirits of the
     dead.

From earliest youth I had been strictly taught
    That ghosts are but a creature of the mind;
Therefore I little cared, and less I thought,
    Among the tombs some horrid fright to find;
But monuments, with cold and silent hearts,
Are things that make the nervous weak; he
     starts;
And yonder apparition assumes a thousand
     parts.

Thick evergreens all through the yard were
     planted,
    Which only helped to make the darkness
     more;
If ever any place on earth was haunted

By spirits coming from the Stygian shore,
'T was there; for, so the story goes around,
At night the passer hears a hideous sound,
Since right beside the path two murdered men
    were found.

I groped my way without a spark of light,
  Till startled by the sound of deathly moan-
    ing,
I stopped and gazed in wonder and in fright,
  For still there came an awful wailing, groan-
    ing,
As of some spirit plunged in deepest woe;
The voice was loud at first, then changed to
    low;
Then died into a whisper, as spirit's, you know.

My hair arose, my voice was in a quiver,
  I trembled like a culprit caught.—E'en now,
At thoughts of that, I feel a sickening shiver,
  A death-like moisture gathers on my brow.—
My tones were strange; although I strove to
    speak,
My answer was a groan, or half a shriek;
I scarcely moved a limb, I felt so very weak.

With throbbing heart half leaping from my
    breast,
  I moved along, with hands the pathway feel-
    ing;

With vivid fancies and with fears possessed,
  But reason and the senses little reeling.
Some feet ahead an untrimmed cedar grew,
The groans came from beneath its boughs, I
        knew,
But nothing could be seen, no form appeared
        in view.

The more I gazed the darker seemed the
        night;
  When, as it were, from out the very ground,
At least I thought so in my foolish fright,
  There came again that same unearthly sound;
Just then, in all sincerity I prayed,
Though often from my early teachings strayed,
By that abiding faith my courage there was
        stayed.

I wished a light, but wild the nightwind tossed;
  With ready match I bended o'er the place,
When, with a cry as of a spirit lost,
  A clammy hand was thrown across my face;
A something grasped me with a giant's arm
And trailed me down. I cried out in alarm;
I thought it must be satan, I feared no other
        harm.

His hold relaxed, I rose upon my feet,
  But nothing felt, the ground seemed soft and
        level;
I asked whom thus I was decreed to meet,

He answered from the grave, "I am the
    devil!"
I sprang almost, if not, six feet on high;
To meet the gentleman I did not sigh;
Much less, there, all alone, a match of power
    to try.

The wind yet blew by starts, though fast 't was
    dying,
    My hand was trembling, still I struck a light;
When, there, within a sunken grave was lying
    A drunken wretch, in such a horrid plight!
That man had been his parents' hope and pride,
The village belle became his envied bride,
'T were better far for both if long before they'd
    died.

The wedding bells ne'er rang a merrier chime,
    While Fortune with her wand was bending
        o'er,
Than they had rung for them one winter time,
    And that was only ten short years before.
A boy of twelve, my mother stroked my hair,
A truant child I was her greatest care;
"Pray be like him," she said, "life's burden
    nobly bear."

He once had loved, too well, the fatal bowl,
    But years had passed since last from it he
        turned;
His bride would have him drink. He fell,
    poor soul!

By what, from other hands, he would have
    spurned.
He took the glass, and drank the poisoned
    draught,
At which the very demons doubtless laughed;
They saw a noble ship turned to a sinking raft.

You ask of her, the once proud village belle,
    Does she yet live to mourn her husband's fall?
She died a month before—the neighbors tell—
    Of broken heart; she found a pauper's pall.
At last she rests from all her earthly strife,
Another story of a blasted life;
And hers, that sunken grave, that same low
    drunkard's wife.

MEXICO.

Where the Aztec's ancient empire flourished,
'Mid Sierra Madre's valleys nourished,
Lies a nation; 't is a remnant only
Of its former greatness; bleak and lonely
Rise the snowy summits.   Mountains hoary,
As in anger, thunder forth the story
Of the cruel white man; there forever
Seemed the nation sleeping, they were never
Thinking of the tyrant.   All is gone forever.

Land of wonder!   Like a vision stealing
Comes the memory of its people kneeling

At the shrine of custom.   They are changing
Little faster than the mountains ranging
'Round them; but their slumber has been
    broken
By the locomotive; 't is a token
Of the coming that will leave remaining
Only foot-prints; modern ways are gaining,
And of all that's ancient naught will be re-
    maining.

Cities of the latest type, appearing,
Greet the traveler, as his train is nearing
One of recent building; but the people
Clad in their serapes, and each steeple
Of the great cathedrals, all are telling,
Plainly as the rude adobe dwelling,
That an unknown people are around him,
Where the mountain walls have firmly bound
    him;
So he wonders if enchantment can have found
    him.

Haciendas but increase the quaintness
Of the country—words at best are faintness
In description; but the hundred places
Where the tourist goes to see the traces
Of a prehistoric age and nation
Have no equal; while the occupation
Of the natives, and their mode of living,
These, to travel in that land, are giving

Charms and novelty that must delight the
    living.

When some scholar gathers each tradition,
Legends whence *their* minds draw all nu-
    trition,
Will the veil that hides their past be lifted,
For, as yet, their clouds are scarcely rifted.
May their banner floating ever prouder,
Deck their mountains! farther, deeper, louder
Sound their anthems, as the ages rolling
Lift the people! Speed the power controlling
Human action, raising mortals, onward rolling!

THE WIZARD OF THE PLAINS.

A sunburnt plain. great heaps of sand,
    Stretching a thousand miles or more;
A dreary waste of desert land
    With hungry vultures flying o'er;
                And that was all.
A wizard from the wizard clime
    Thrice stretched his wand above the plain,
There rose, an honor to our time,
    Great Kansas with its fields of grain;
                That is not all.
Many have found a home at last,
    To whom the word seemed foreign tongue.

Her people cannot be surpassed,
  Their praise has never yet been sung;
                That is not half.
Saloons, the darkest crimes of man,
  Are banished from the state for aye;
Instead thereof the people plan
  The farmer's home, our country's stay.
                'T is they who laugh.

A PERUVIAN LEGEND.

In the legends of Peru this story is told;
Ere the white man had robbed it of treasures
    of gold,
How the nation was founded in ages long
    flown;
And the Inca first crowned, and then placed
    on the throne.

In a lake in the mountains high up from the
    shore,
It said that an island with volcanic roar
In a moment arose, and the waters receding
Left the island alone, and the wild birds there
    feeding.

O'er the mountains the sun was just ready to
    break,

When a vessel of lightning appeared on the
　　lake;
And it sailed toward the isle, Titicaca by name,
While from midst of the lightning a fire-figure
　　came.

It was Manco Capac who stepped forth on the
　　strand,
Stood with one foot on water, the other on land;
Stretched one hand to southward, to northward
　　stretched one,
Turned his face toward the east, and gazed
　　long on the sun.

With his right hand still toward Illimani on high,
And his left toward Sorata that towers to the
　　sky,
There fell from the heavens a scepter and
　　sword,
And they hung in the air by the power of the
　　Lord.

"Come ye forth, come ye forth!" thrice he
　　cried out aloud,
When descending direct from an o'erhanging
　　cloud,
Came a woman whose features were kindness
　　and love,
While the thunders were rolling in grandeur
　　above.

In a moment advancing, he stood at her side,
While her garments betold that she came as a
  bride;
And a crown formed of gold and of silver, they
  vow,
Coming down from above twice encircled each
  brow.

A throne then arose by the same secret force,
And courtiers flocked 'round as a matter of
  course.
Thus tell they the story, at least it is one,
Of that west land of light where they worship
  the sun.

THE AZTEC'S LAMENT.

TRANSLATED FROM A MEXICAN MS., SAID TO
HAVE BEEN WRITTEN AFTER THE TREATY
OF 1848.

They came from the north, all secure in their
  might,
  Like hawks that are hungry swoop down on
    their prey;
No condor was ever more swift in his flight,
  No eagle, more fierce in her onslaught than
    they.

Their step like a blight spread destruction
  before;

No power could withstand them, no force
    could repel;
To retreat was in vain, and in vain to implore,
    The brave of our land by their eagerness fell.

We knew at the first, when the armies marched
    forth,
    That their cannons were true, and that sharp
        was their sword;
But little we thought that the states of the
    North
    Would rush o'er our land like a barbarous
        horde.

No terms could appease them, no peace could
    we make,
    They were marching with hopes and resolves
        running high;
Not even tenfold were they willing to take,
    The share of the cougar would not satisfy.

On, on, marched their legions like tyrants
    of old,
    Notwithstanding our arms, though right
        nobly they fought;
They robbed, for, in fact, the poor pittance of
    gold
    Was nothing compared to the land that they
        got.

The Christian, that tells of his mercy and love,

And had taught the poor Aztec to think him
    sincere,
Every mercy forgot, for his greed was above
    All his notions of right, and his heart—ah,
    how sear!

Go, then, to your homes, with your banners all
    spread,
    And the blood of your victims still warm on
    your spears;
Your triumph is full, if ye count not the dead,
    And as sweet is man's sleep without sorrow-
    ing tears.

Proud states of the North, by the bones of
    your slain,
    You have robbed in a manner beneath a
    great foe;
For the cry of your slave and the clank of his
    chains
    You have spread your domain, but 't will end
    in your woe!

THE IMMIGRANT'S WIFE.

A weary woman longed and sighed
    For her ancestral bowers,
Until beside the road she spied
    Two tiny prairie flowers.

They turned the current of her thoughts
　　And woke her better cheer;
"If these two wild forget-me-nots
　　Can bloom so brightly here,

"It brings me to a sense of right,
　　No more I'll sighing brood."
From that her heart was always light;
　　She sang in merry mood.

Her home is still upon the plains;
　　A cheerful, happy wife,
She sings like lark in morning strains;
　　So full of hope and life.

From lowly flowers we all may learn,
　　If we are so inclined.
Of life, the greatest joys we earn—
　　They are in peace of mind.

TO A PUPIL.

May the lessons I have taught you
　　Be to you a source of pleasure;
In one fault I never caught you,
　　Hoarding up an earthly treasure;
But I beg you, need I tell it?
Follow wisdom like a zealot;
Hoard it like a miser's coffers,
Notwithstanding idle scoffers.

TO A LADY.

The ladies and roses were given to man,
  To cheer, and to lighten his burden of care;
They fill their appointment—deny it who
    can—
  As nothing else does, the two angels so fair.

THE WINDS.

Last night, I sat within my study reading
  The story of the wars of ancient ages;
Weary with care and toil, and yet unheeding
  The call to rest, I read the bloody pages;
But nature conquers all, I soon was sleeping,
A strange unhappy feeling o'er me creeping;
I heard a maniac laugh, and then a voice of
    weeping.

The prairie winds, so loved in hours of waking,
  Whose every tone is music to our people,
Sang wild discordant songs, my slumber break-
    ing
  With moanings, as they whistled through the
    steeple

Of the village church; and then again, their
    sighing
Grew faint, until within the distance dying,
Much like the rending wail of some fond sis-
    ter crying.

I was a child; they soothed my youthful slumb-
    bers
  With mellow songs, as of an angel mother.
No other voice can sing in hallowed numbers
  With half a mother's sweetness—no, none
    other.
No other hand can cool the fevered pillow,
No other power can quell the stormy billow,
I was a prattling child beneath my favorite
    willow.

The winds now changed, their tone was one of
    laughter,
  I was a boy at play with boisterous shouting,
Or roving through the wood the farm dog after,
  Some luckless wood-chuck or opossum rout-
    ing;
At night around the family hearthstone playing;
The eve now spent, an aged sire is praying;
Oh could I lean as he, upon that Power so
    staying!

Once more they sang, in accents slow and
    measured,

Yet strong, like manhood in his hour of
    glory:
"They quickly fly, the moments you have
    treasured;
  How soon the child will tremble, aged and
    hoary!
Be bold, be strong, man's dearest rights de-
    fending,
The youth are on thy power and strength
    depending,
To elevate mankind thy loyal efforts lending."

With trembling step, and weak with time and
    sorrow,
  The withered remnant of a generation,
I saw myself; they sang of my to-morrow
  And of a place redeemed from lamentation.
How cold and desolate, when death is near us,
To gaze beyond, without a hope to cheer us,
To feel that if we call, no ear awaits to hear us!

Again, I heard the church bell's solemn tolling,
  I saw the plumes upon my dark hearse wav-
    ing,
Each mournful sound seemed o'er and o'er me
    rolling,
  Like ocean waves when shipwrecked victim
    craving.
I heard the clods upon my coffin falling,
Whose hollow sounds were frightful and
    appalling,

I heard great Gabriel's trump the world to
    judgment calling.

I started up, and looked around in wonder,
    I shook myself to stir my powers of thinking;
Without, the lightnings flashed, with distant
    thunder;
    I staggered when I walked as if from drink-
    ing.
My dream was done.   Like dreams this life
    is fleeing,
The spark dies out, it ends our earthly being;
What lies beyond this vale, we have no power
    of seeing.

MEXICAN LEGENDS.

THE FLOWERS.

In the springtime of creation,
  Though the summer brought the showers,
And the grass grew in abundance,
  Earth produced no kind of flowers.

In the grave a child they buried,
  Once so innocent and bright;
From her tomb the flowers sprang blooming,
  But alas! they all were white.

In the evening came the mother, ·
  Came to weep above her dead;
On the flowers her tears were sprinkled,
  And behold! they turned to red.

As the shades of night grew thicker,
  Heavy fell the summer dew;
When the morning sun had risen
  Some were red and some were blue.

Time and season mixed the colors,
  Spread the flowers on every hand;
But the ones of richest mixture
  Grow within their native land.

3

Flowers are emblems of earth's beauty,
  And their colors only show
What a wealth of love undying
  Mother's tender heart can know.

THE VOLCANOES.

When creation's work was finished,
  Sorrow was unknown to all
Till the evil spirits tempted,
  And they wrought the mortal's fall.

Evil spirits, bolder growing,
  Led the human race still lower;
Till the Father, waxing angry,
  Could, and would, endure no more.

Then his strongest angels coming,
  Tore the mountains from their base,
Rolled the spirits down beneath them,
  Upward turning each one's face;

Turned the mountains back upon them,
  Hold them safely fastened in;
Will not let them die, nor free them,
  Till the mortals cease to sin.

Now, the spirits have repented,
  And they speak to warn mankind;
Only speak with voice of warning,
  That is all the tongue they find.

When the people grow too wicked,
   Then the buried spirits groan;
Belch the fire from out the mountains;
   Turning, writhe and heave and moan.

Lofty Popocatapetl
   Holds the wicked leader fast;
When from bondage they are loosened
   He will not be freed till last.

This is why the mountains burning,
   Send their darting flames on high;
That the people may take warning,
   As the glare illumes the sky.

THE WAR CLOUD.

1885.

O Europe, boasted land of art and arms,
   The home of science and the seat of lore.
What mean these marshalled hosts, these
      strange alarms,
   That earth should echo with the cannons'
      roar,
   And peace again forsake thy proud, historic
      shore?

Why are the war clouds gathering in the East?
   They tell of fields of carnage and of gore,
While dreaded Moloch waits but for a feast,

To drink thy noblest blood and cry for more,
And in thy armies' trail go rushing as of
    yore.

O Russia, with thy almost boundless fields,
  Whose equal scarcely can on earth be seen,
Remember that the fruit the battle yields
  Will dye with red the plains now growing
    green,
  And that, to thee is most the gathering war
    clouds mean.

Proud Britain, boasted mistress of the sea,
  The richest isle that decks the earth, by far.
What tales of victory or woe to thee
  Are in those clouds, the lowering clouds of
    war,
  So soon to shake the earth beneath the battle
    car ?

Thy knightly sons will leave their stately halls,
  And go to battle in a foreign land;
Thy cottage sons will leave their lowly walls,
  And cast their lots upon a foreign strand;
  And Death go forth to reap, and gather
    home thy band.

For thee and thy success we humbly pray,
  For Europe's hope lies in Britannia's sword;
Slavonic rule is but barbaric sway,

And all but thee seem fearful of his horde;
But thou canst win alone, the price thou
    must afford.

Wields man no higher power than low-born
    brutes,
    Like hungry wolves that fight upon the
       plain?
Of all that man has learned, are these the
    fruits:
    To war? Then go and gaze upon the slain,
    And make thy boast no more, for thou hast
       learned in vain.

The time when men should war has long since
    passed,
    The arbitration of the sword is old;
The time will come, ay, surely come at last,
    When human lives will not be bought and
       sold
    To satisfy a king; their worth is more than
       gold.

Columbia, far removed from these, to thee
    We look in pride; thou art the land of light,
No other nation ever was so free.
    Long mayst thou live the guardian of the
       right,
    And each successive age but make thy stars
       more bright!

SOUTH AMERICA.

South of us lies a peninsula,
  Wide in its pampas and river,
Rich in its sylvas and mineral,
  Blessed by the hand of the Giver.

Mostly unchanged by humanity,
  Just as it was at creation;
Great in its mountains, and promising
  Scene of a forthcoming nation.

Not by the arm of the conqueror,
  Not by the battle's commotion;
But from the native inhabitants
  Rising, like mist from the ocean.

Catching the breath of our hurricane,
  Rush of their northern neighbor;
Soon will you hear them exultingly
  Singing the chorus of labor.

In the upbuilding futurity,
  Wise be the councils prevailing,
Founding on precepts republican;
  Friendly, the winds, to their sailing.

When they awake from their listlessness—
  And of a surety they're waking;

Butterflies leaving the chrysalis,
  Never were quicker in breaking.

Travelers seeking the wonderful,
  Never, there, feel themselves weary;
Never, there, know a satiety;
  Never can think of the dreary:

If they but study with diligence,
  If they but turn their attention,
Seeking the places so numerous
  Worthy, but lengthy to mention.

Mention? when man never heard of them,
  Places whose names never spoken;
Many, where eyes never looked on them,
  Stillness, by human unbroken.

People whose methods are primitive,
  Worthy the painter and writer;
Catching the rays from Columbia,
  Soon will their country be brighter.

Peace guard their borders unceasingly,
  Green be the huacal grass growing,
Joy crown their hearthstones unstintedly,
  Harvests grow rich for their sowing!

THE RICH MAN'S DREAM.

A man of wealth, who long had drunk
   His joys from Fashion's golden boards,
Had once become completely sunk
   Below the peace this earth affords.
Of these he said, "For all they give,
I do not wish to longer live."

Upon his costly couch he slept,
   And dreaming, saw a spirit stand;
He thought his mother o'er him wept,
   And stroked his hair with silken hand.
The angel said, "They live in vain
Who never heed the cry of pain."

He waking took a lengthy stroll
   Until he reached a hovel door;
He entering, saw with troubled soul,
   A woman sick upon the floor.
Her hungry children cowered and shrank,
The husband and the father drank.

The rich man had her kindly nursed,
   Had all removed from den of gloom,
To where the cheering sunlight burst
   Like angel's visit through the room;

He helped the drunken man to rise,
And held him up, to men's surprise.

He saw a struggling genius stand,
   And try to mount fate's rugged wall;
He gave him gold, he took his hand,
   And helped him till he need not fall;
For genius is not apt to sport
Where Mammon holds his gorgeous court.

The wealthy man from that day on,
   Appeared to live alone for others.
He mourned his life so nearly gone
   Before he learned that all are brothers.
When next the angels' voice he hears,
They 'll waft his soul to brighter spheres.

A FADED FLOWER.

It is a withered rose,
   A little faded flower,
On which I love to gaze
   In quiet evening hour.

One morning long ago
   My way to school I took;
My father plucked the flower
   And placed it in my book.

We met upon the road,
    The rose was growing wild;
He brought to me the flower,
    And blessed his little child.

The book and rose are worn,
    The father gone to rest;
No wonder that the flower
    My lips have often pressed.

THE NINETEENTH CENTURY.

MAY, 1887.

The centuries are leaves in Time's great book,
    Men's lives, the letters for the printed page;
Some lives are head-lines, and for some we
       look
In vain; they are the leading for their age.
The noblest lives are sometimes scarcely found,
    A foot-note brief, unnoticed by the world;
But in that book each leaf is firmly bound.
    However strong Time's ruthless tempest
       whirled,
    No record has been lost, though lives to ruin
       hurled.

Ye living men, when this our page is done
    What shall it be?   The closing years are
       here;

There 's much to do, great works scarce yet
    begun,
  For giants tremble with a pigmy's fear.
Great Europe, burdened with her mighty load,
  Is slowly waking to the rights of man;
But Russia stands a mountain in the road,
   While others lead in an uncertain plan;
    Yet all are far behind our own unswerving
    van.

A land of schools and homes, like ours, should
    rise
   And break the fetters that have bound the
   past
Barbaric times.   It needs no prophet's eyes
  To see a better era coming fast.
Ours is the brightest century of time;
  But may the years yet left exceed the whole
Of that now gone.   The slimy sea of crime,
   Saloon's dark gulf, where murky billows roll,
   Should be at least walled in ere time your
   knell shall toll.

The schools for homeless, and asylums, show
  Man's nobler nature, and we gaze in awe;
But when we see the cities' crime and woe,
  And know that it is sanctioned by the law,
We wonder, what is man?   The people pay
  A heavy tax in nearly every state;
And yet, 't is almost wholly thrown away

To keep the dramshops' crew.   The people
      prate
About their liberties; such liberties *men* hate.

That men should seek to elevate the race,
  And see a viper gnawing at its heart,
Yet shield the poisoned serpent in its place,
  Is playing either knaves' or cowards' part.
That state alone is free, where every wrong
  That threatens innocence and youth with ill
Is seized, with gentle hands, albeit strong,
  And placed beneath the bane of moral will
  Until it 's ground to dust, like wheat in flour-
      ing mill.

While Europe pours her scum upon our shore,
  Mere vassals to some foreign prince or
      power,
To drive the laborers' wages lower and lower,
  And help retard Hope's great triumphal
      hour,
The people calmly sit and wait, for what?
  Simply to see our country overflow
With men who seek to set our laws at naught.
  Their coming is to all that 's good, a blow;
  And moral cowardice alone permits it so.

Awake, awake, O power that lifts mankind!
  Assert thy strength, protect our country
      broad!
Display in man that attribute of mind
  Which tends to lift the mortal from the sod!

The nineteenth century is near its close,
    What shall the stories of its last years be?
They must be even brighter far than those
    Now gone to sink in time's unfathomed sea.
    O, make our people strong! themselves they
        must make free.

THE SOLDIERS' HOME IN KANSAS.
1885.

Workmen, lay well the corner-stone,
    And rear the turret high;
Ye build for Freedom and her own
    Beneath the freemen's sky.
Gray hairs will soon bedeck each brow
    That heard the battle-call;
But ah, how many have ere now
    Been borne upon the pall!

When man is young and in his might,
    He laughs at care and want;
But when he nears Death's silent night
    They seem a spectre gaunt.
Then build ye well their earthly home,
    They are a noble band;
Compelled by want, they should not roam
    Who fought to save our land.

And yet, to call it home is wrong,
   For love must needs be there,
Where mother sings her matchless song,
   And father kneels in prayer;
Or where a wife's fond hands are found
   To soothe the brow of care;
Her love will help to heal each wound—
   Home only can be there!

Come, build ye well each silent wall
   That shelters from the cold;
For countless evils can befall
   The poor, the lame, the old;
And all that man can give them here
   Our debt will not repay;
But words of love will surely cheer
   Them on their lonely way.

Twice welcome, soldiers, to our state,
   All honor to your band!
To you we gladly dedicate
   This beauteous piece of land.
May long and happy be the years
   Yet spared to you below;
And bliss beyond this vale of tears
   When ye are called to go!

With pride the Kansan looks abroad
   Upon our boundless plain;
And then, with thanks looks up to God,
   Who gives us sun and rain;

Then thinks of fields where grows the rice—
   New England's sterile coast;
They all are his, he paid the price,
   Our Nation is his boast.

Then welcome, soldiers, once again!
   Alike from whence ye came,
We only care that ye are men
   Who share the patriot's fame.
The gallant chieftain of our state
   Is of your number true,
And gladly will he dedicate
   This hallowed spot to you.
May Heaven look down and bless alway
   The red, the white, the blue!

ON THE DEATH OF PRESIDENT GRANT.

1885.

Away, away from the fields of care,
   Hushed be the sound of the busy surge!
The voice of mourning is filling the air—
   The people are singing their hero's dirge.
Dear to the hearts alike of them all,
Beloved in the cottage, extolled in the hall,
He wakes no more at the morning's call,
But sleeps to-day 'mid the silent throng
Of those who, departed, live ever in song.

All nations have had their heroes tried,
   Of whom they boast in studied phrase:
" Lo! for his land he lived, or died "—
   And vie to sing their chieftains' praise.
Statesman and warrior, both was he;
   Unequalled in his age or clime,
And his the land of liberty,
   And his the matchless modern time.

In vain the praise of tongue or pen,
He'll hear no earthly sound again;
But while a loving people keep
Their watch and ward, sometimes to weep,
' T is fitting that his praise be sung
By every patriotic tongue;
For so we teach the youthful heart
To live and love the patriot's part.

Full many a place upon the earth
   Is hallowed by its human clay;
Here sleeps a son of lowly birth,
   As noble, grand, as true as they.
His tomb will be a sacred shrine,
'Round which the people will entwine
The wreathes that are the sure reward
Of those who stand as Freedom's guard.

Slowly and sadly the funeral train
Moves to the sound of the muffled strain.
Who are the mourners? Ay, every one
That dwells in the land of the setting sun:

And many who live beyond the wave,
Would deck with flowers, if they could, his
    grave.
Inscribe on his tomb no long-drawn phrase,
For few were his words, and simple his ways;
Some lowly lines, as, " He lived and he died
Beloved by mankind and his country's pride."

THE GRAVE OF KEOKUK.

'Tis near this spot, no matter where,
    That Keokuk, the chief, is lying;
Perhaps it is for him the winds
    Amid those trees are sadly sighing.

Pursued like fox throughout his life:
    The grave—why should it not provide him
With that sweet rest that life denied,
    Or rather that the whites denied him?

Vain be your search to find his bones,
    Ye cruel men, his sleep is better
Than in your great museum's wall;
    His limbs in life you could not fetter.

.CUPID AND THE CANNON.

CUPID AND THE CANNON.

A TALE OF THE REBELLION.

Sometimes in idle hours, will rhymes unsought
  Arrange themselves in some romantic lay;
The which, as things unfitting graver thought,
  Are burnt or blotted on some wiser day.
These few survive, and, truly let me say,
  Court not the critic's smile, nor dread his frown;
Perchance they 'll serve to while an hour away.
  Nor does the volume ask for more renown
  Than Ennui's yawning smile, what time she
    drops it down.

Adapted from Scott.

CUPID AND THE CANNON.

CHAPTER FIRST.

THE PLANTER.

Duke—And what's her history?
Vio.—A blank, my lord. She never told her love;
    But let concealment, like a worm i' the bud,
  Feed on her damask cheeks.
                        —*Shakespeare.*

    O fair young land! the youngest, fairest far
      Of which our world can boast,
  Whose guardian planet, evening's silver star,
    Illumes thy golden coast.
                        —*Taylor.*

I.

Far reaching from Atlantic's shore,
Where wild waves toss with hollow roar;
Over the eastern mountain chains;
Across the midland hills and plains;
Over the Rockies steep and wild,
Where winds are fierce, and vales are mild,
Down to the smooth Pacific's side,
Stretches a nation far and wide,
The flower of the West, the patriot's pride.
It reaches north to the fields of snow,
Where the winter winds in their fury blow;
And south to the clime where the orange
  grows,

And all unknown are frosts and snows.
But turn to the years that have fled away,
For life is short as a winter day.

II.

O proud Republic of the West,
Beloved by man, by Heaven blessed;
'Tis well, by times to sing thy songs;
To praise the right, forget thy wrongs;
To sing a dirge with those who weep
O'er graves where fallen heroes sleep;
To sing the songs that freedom wakes
From southern gulf to northern lakes.
Thy struggles and thy triumphs are
Fit theme for lay of love or war,
Since o'er our land on pinions bright,
The White-winged Dove betakes her flight;
The olive branch unsullied now,
She plants on plain and mountain brow.
A nation where the people reign
Deserves by far a nobler strain;
Yet all for thee, for thee and thine;
Long may thy stars in glory shine !

III.

Amidst Virginia's hills of green
A planter's mansion may be seen;
Not far from where the river New
Flows westward from the chain of Blue,
Then breaks the Alleghanies through.

Of noble blood the planter came,
Of house once known to power and fame.
The story of his grandsire's birth
Is known and read o'er half the earth;
So pardon, while our humble rhymes
Rehearse that tale of early times.
'T is to those scenes our lines are turned,
    The days that are of yore,
When many a red man's camp-fire burned,
And pipe of peace the white man spurned,
    Along Atlantic's shore.

IV.

Beneath a great primeval wood,
    A band of savage men lay round;
With double guard the white man stood,
    His wrists with cutting fetters bound.
For days the savage band had cried,
    In scenes of wild and hideous revel;
While some more wise, perhaps, had tried
With magic wand, with magic rod,
    To see if he was of the devil,
Or if, perchance, he came a god.
At last the fatal fire was started
    Within the council hall;
The bands upon his wrists were parted
    When in the council wall.

V.

The hall was built of boughs of oak,
    Without a corner stone,

And woodman ne'er had dealt a stroke
    Upon the monarch's throne.
His kingly garb looked strange, no doubt,
    Though surely thick and strong;
Of raccoon skin with hair turned out,
    And sewed with hickory thong.
A crown of feathers in a band,
    Upon his head he wore;
A maiden sat on either hand,
    The council fire before;
The warriors stood in double file,
    Two hundred armed and strong;
The women gathered round, the while,
    And swelled the eager throng.

VI.

The council soon drew to a close,
    The captive doomed to die;
At that he slowly, calmly rose,
    Nor heaved a long-drawn sigh.
They bound, and laid him on a stone,
    While he in silence prayed.
The chief still sat upon his throne,
    And every sound was stayed;
When forward sprang a maiden grave,
    A daughter of the chief;
His life she begged her sire to save,
    And seemed in deepest grief.

VII.

O woman, strange the power you wield,
  For good or evil as you may;
You make the soldier take his shield,
  And rush to mingle in the fray;
You bid the monarch on his throne,
  Bow humbly at your shrine,
In stately hall, in every zone,
  Beneath the wildwood vine.
Go, white man, you are spared to-day,
  For woman breaks your thongs;
Too oft, alas! she leads astray,
  Yet more she rights man's wrongs.

VIII.

Among the whites a scion stayed,
  Of lordly English blood;
He wooed the wild, untutored maid,
  The daughter of the Wood.
He taught her of the human weal
  That looks to realms above;
Until she at the font could kneel,
  And plight her Savior's love.
The April sun still shone aslant,
  The song of bird was shrill,
When from the church a wedding chant
  Was borne from hill to hill.
Thus, he, the favored Saxon son,
And she, the Indian maid, were one,
  For good or for the ill.

IX.

Descended of this worthy pair,
Is he who occupies our care.—
His name?   Perhaps 't is best untold,
For still he lives, though growing old;
So call him General Blair.
A true Virginia son is he,
And proud of his ancestral line;
His tables creak with richest wine;
Of chivalry he makes his boast;
In sooth he is a worthy host,
And each and every guest makes free.—
A hundred slaves toiled day by day,
That he might lead a genteel life.
Thus wore his days, his years away,
With pleasures wild, yet fraught with strife.

X.

Not so with his good wife, by far:
  She was of old New England stock.
Though time our early hopes may mar,
  Youth's lessons last like mountain rock.
Since men would leave their native soil
  To find a home beyond the wave;
Endure privation, want, and toil,
  Nor shrink before the yawning grave;
Thus, brave the perils of the deep,
  And break the wild, the stubborn sod;
Midst frontier perils calmly sleep,

Relying on the care of God:
Scarce need we say, that where such men
  Can wield the power that makes the state,
Crime only, leads to prison den;
  That none are slaves, and none born great.

XI.

It is not strange that she, who learned
  The lesson of her childhood's years,
Where most by toil their bread have earned,
  And all unknown are slaves' sad tears,
Should sometimes kneel with streaming eyes,
  And pray to God who rules o'er all,
To hear the bondsman's mournful cries,
  And break the bands that cause his thrall.

XII.

They had a daughter, young and fair,
On whom they lavished all their care;
In wisdom she was not a sage,
But, like all others of her age,
She dreamed the visions wild of youth;
But all have done the same, in truth.
Few children of our free-born race,
Who have not built in empty space,
A castle great, perhaps more grand
Than ever built by human hand.
Then laugh not at the childish dream
That sees this life a silver stream;
For all too soon, the child must know

Those castles fade like spring time snow;
That silver stream of youthful years
Has no supply save bitter tears.

XIII.

'T was thus with her of whom we write,
She saw this life as noon-day bright;
Nor cared for much save mirth and play,
Through winter eve and summer day;
Though rich was she, and all must know
That riches sway a power below.
Beyond the broad Atlantic's tide,
A kindred, on the day he died,
Had left her land, and gold in store,
Ten thousand pounds or even more.

XIV.

Evil and homely are the faces
From which wealth cannot wipe all traces.
Since she was fair, with winning smiles,
It is not strange the suitors' wiles
Were tried, but all in vain were they;
With cold disdain she turned away.
Two found *some* favor with the maid,
Who also did with parents staid,
    With one or with the other;
The father favored one the more,
And made him welcome doubly o'er,
    But not so with the mother.

XV.

The one dwelt where the river James
    Flows by a city fair and old;
'T is Richmond 'mong historic names,
    But more of it need not be told.
He, too, came of that fiery blood
    That marked the Old Dominion most;
When crossed, it rose like angry flood,
    And valor was each planter's boast.
That ancient spirit in him grew,
As evil habits sometimes do.
Jealous of insult, proud of name,
Was Harold Lee—he is the same.

XVI.

The mother, as we may suppose,
    Looked not so kindly on the suit;
For she was reared and taught by those
    Who held all men above the brute.—
And so they are by nature's touch;
    But drink is full of bitter woe,
And some love Mammon all too much;
    For each, men sink, the beast below.—
She rather chose to favor one
    Whose lineage was from Pilgrim sires;
For so our human natures run;
    Time often strengthens youth's desires.

XVII.

His parents dwelt not far from where
    The Laurel mountain summits rise

And look upon three states; 't is there
   He learned to love his native skies.
No slave should toil, that he might live
The life that wealth alone can give.
His talents were to books inclined,
His treasures were in strength of mind.
He strove to live and do the right—
Untitled name, plain Norman White.
It is not strange that he should care
To win the hand of Laura Blair.

XVIII.

Laura, with kindness looked on each;
   Nor seemed her fickle mind to know;
The lessons that the heart should teach,
   To learn, she seemed extremely slow.
A mother's smile, a father's frown,
   But made her doubt herself the more;
Each rising hope was smothered down,
   And she was weaker than before.
In this respect, and this alone,
   In others she took well her part.
She was a child scarce fully grown,
   Yet hers a worthy hand and heart.

XIX.

Two lovers of the same fair maid
Were never friends, in truth was said;
Without exception 't is the rule
Alike of men, and lads at school.

Then think not strange we must relate
The rising of a deadly hate;
When youthful blood is running warm
None can presage the coming storm.
The storms of life are largely brought
Upon ourselves; though life is fraught
With many cares, what peace to find
Our every hope on faith reclined!

XX.

The planter loved the chase and hound,
To him the bay was welcome sound.
When Christmas with its round of mirth
Was soon to come, and snow-decked earth
Gave promise of a royal chase,
He gathered many to his place.
The summer, he had been away,
But now was home, a month to stay,
A week of merry sport to give,
For such the life he chose to live.

XXI.

The morning dawned, the sun's first streak
Was bursting o'er the mountain-peak,
When Harold, with his dog and gun,
Had sallied forth to meet the sun;
And Norman, just the night before,
Had landed at the planter's door;
For many a one from far and near,
Oft came to spend a fortnight here.

Both youth and maid, as we are told,
To come and stay were ever bold;
The table always spread full wide
With merry guests on either side.

XXII.

The other, too, rose with the light—
It was a morning clear and bright—
He merely wandered out awhile
The early morning to beguile;
But soon the two met face to face
Alone in a secluded place.
Harold, a duel sought and found,
They chose the weapons and the ground;
Down where the little brooklet flows,
Where that great ancient oak tree grows,
  By yonder second hill;
To-morrow morning just at eight—
Each pledged himself the time to wait—
  They are to try their skill.

CUPID AND THE CANNON.

CHAPTER SECOND.

WAR.

But whether on the scaffold high,
  Or in the battle's van,
The fittest place where man can die
  Is where he dies for man.
                              —*M. F. Barry.*

" Prithee tell me, Dimple-Chin,
At what age does Love begin?
Your blue eyes have scarcely seen
Summers three, my fairy queen."
        *   *   *   *
"Oh!" the rosy lips reply,
" I can't tell you, if I try.
'T is so long I can't remember,
Ask some younger lass than I."
                              —*Stedman.*

I.

The grass grows green on every hill,
And merrily laughs the little rill;
The wild bird sings in sweetest strain
'Midst forest pines in far off Maine;
Those joyous songs of brook and bird
From all New England's bounds are heard;
Mingled with hum of human throng,
That help to swell our country's song.
  5

Great ships of every nation ride
Upon the ocean's changing tide,
Along her shores and in her ports;
There, men know naught of regal courts,
But only bow before the throne
Of Him who calls the world His own.

II.

There, all are hardy sons of toil,
Taught by their clime, their stubborn soil.
The proudest title of the land
Is earned by toil of brain or hand.
Their sterile soil, their rugged clime,
They thrice repair with well spent time.
When sunny summer days are o'er,
And wild winds howl around the door,
The farmer bids the storm to blow,
Unmindful of the drifting snow.
His barns are filled with needed grain,
And proof against all storm and rain;
Warm is his house, and rich the store
That lies within his pantry door.
Contentment rules within his home;
His children do not long to roam
Out where the world its snare has spread,
And gilded lights their false rays shed;
But well have learned that peace and love
Will make a home like heaven above.

III.

It seems, as we hear the ocean's roar,
As it beats and lashes against the shore,
That the waves of Time thus rock and rave
As if to hasten us on to the grave.
Yet, who can adjudge them to be but good,
When he thinks of the thousands that toil for
    food,
With a garret home and a rude straw bed,
And their only food the coarsest bread?
On city street, with naught to eat,
How many children roam each night!
In every city, with none to pity,
Homeless and friendless, the night seems
    endless,
In the pitiless storm, with shivering form,
They dread the night with its snows so white;
But may the grave with its silent wave
Soon bear them away to the Land of Light.

IV.

The Land of Light, how fair it must be,
Compared to earth and the scenes we see!
But back on the years of the past we gaze:
Alas, for man and his cruel ways!
Yet green be the graves of friend and of foe,
And bright be the flowers on each mound that
    grow;
If the spot is unmarked, may the wild lilies
    blow.

v.

The Northland lay in its peace and pride,
And plenty reigned on every side;
Rich was the harvest the fields brought forth,
Through all the states of the busy North.
The farmer toiled through the livelong day,
Laying his winter store away;
He plied the plow, the reaper, run;
Sowing and reaping from sun to sun;
For well he knew, in a land of snow,
That all who eat must toil as they go.
Over the cities hung clouds of smoke,
Hiding the sun with their sable cloak;
While the humming noise of busy mills
Was heard afar o'er the eastern hills;
And countless flocks and herds were seen,
Roaming through valleys rich and green.

vi.

Westward, the sound of the pioneer
Was mingled with that of the fleeing deer;
And cities, as if by magic, sprung
Where yet the sound of the huntsman rung.
But turn to the South, and you see no more
The scenes you saw on the North lake shore;
Cities were few, and small were they,
That dotted the Southland far away.
Plantations spreading far and wide
Betold the southern planter's pride;

For here, in luxury and ease,
Seeking himself alone to please,
The haughty planter's life was spent,
On earthly pleasures only bent;
While poor slave's cry of dread despair
Rose nightly on the balmy air;
As if to God for vengeance cried,
And all unwept the bondsman died.

VII.

At last the wrath of Heaven awoke,
And God hurled down his thunder stroke.
Abaddon raised his horrid hand,
And Azrael stalked across the land.
   Each smiled to see the baleful hour,
   Destined to try a nation's power;
For time's great waves forever roll,
Unmindful though the death knell toll
   And thickening war clouds lower.
Man, with his boasted skill and strength,
Of time can not extend the length;
With all his power, with all his pride,
Of time he ne'er can turn the tide.
Those ceaseless waves forever roll
   His bark toward yonder shore;
Until one mightier than the rest,
Shall lift him high upon its breast;
He sees his sun set in the west,
   He hears the breakers roar.

Hark ye! there is a deadlier sound
Re-echoing through the hills around,
At which each patriot's heart must bound,
Than e'en the wild waves' roar,
Or breakers on the shore.

VIII.

It sounds again, and louder far,
It is the thunder peal of war;
And see, the stars and stripes must fall!
Alas, alas! I know it all.
No, no! there sleeps on Vernon's hill
A sainted form, though cold and still;
On many an eastern hillside, too,
There sleeps a patriot, tried and true.
Within the grave their very bones
Would wake and writhe with hollow groans,
Or horrid skeletons would tread
O'er all the land, not lie as dead,
If, when a foe that flag should dare,
No voice of vengeance fills the air;
If hosts of heroes would not spring
Swifter than bird of prey on wing,
To raise the banner, or to die
That it might float again on high.

IX.

Alas, that Heaven's chosen land
Should tremble at the battle brand;
That the reveille's sound should wake

The sleeping echoes; or should break
The brooding stillness of the years,
And fill the hearts with hopes and fears!
See Freedom's banner trailed in dust!
Awake, O Nation! or you must,
When at the last you wake in vain,
Behold our country rent in twain.
Since first the day when war began
To be the highest court of man,
A braver foe has never trod
Where battle-blood has dyed the sod.

x.

Scarce had the morning sun's first light
Dispelled the dark and gloom of night,
When on the breeze, as thunder roar,
Was borne the news to every door.
Swift as the forked lightning flies
On summer evening through the skies,
The mighty cities' noise and jar
Were hushed to hear the news of war.
From stately hall where wealthy dwell,
From humble cot in lowly dell,
Men vied, to see who first should go
To meet upon the field the foe;
And women, bravest on the sphere,
Bade husbands swell the Union cheer;
While mothers—Heaven bless them all—
Bade sons to conquer or to fall;

And maidens, with a parting sigh,
Sent lovers forth to win or die.

XI.

Though trembling was the mother's voice,
   The maiden's eyes bedimmed with tears,
They knew and made the patriot's choice,
   Their loyal love o'ercame their fears.
Many the sons of foreign land,
From Emerald Isle to Grecian strand;
From where the mighty Danube flows,
To Norway's fields of ice and snows;
Adopted children by our laws,
Who nobly helped the Nation's cause.
In lowly cot, in gilded hall,
Was heard alike our country's call,
And men of every age and state,
Alike the humble and the great,
Were crowding in a common car,
And rushing to the scenes of war;
While songs that cheer the patriot's soul,
Above the battle thunders roll.

XII.

SONG.

The eagle is mounting supreme in his flight,
The star spangled banner is borne to the light,
The symbol of strength and the emblem of
      right;

May the home and the field be our sword and
　　our shield,
　And the workman's right arm be our forts.
May the press and the school help the people
　　to rule,
　For we wish not the king and his courts.

Our freedom was bought with the blood of the
　　brave,
For our fathers chose death to the life of the
　　slave;
May we stand like a guard 'round each pa-
　　triot's grave.

May the old eagle's home still be built in each
　　dome
Of our land, and the star spangled banner still
　　wave.

May the proud eagle soar o'er Columbia's
　　shore .
　Till the angel of time shall have flown;
And alone, Death shall stand on the sea and
　　on land,
　And proclaim that the earth is his own.

XIII.

Too far our rambling tale has pressed
From where the planter cheered his guest.
The morning sun had once again
Lit up the hill, the wood, the glen;
The hands that marked the dial plate

Were pressing hard the hour of eight,
When Laura, safe in morning nap,
Was startled by an anxious rap.
The door unlocked, a watchful nurse
Revealed the truth; she made it worse,
Perhaps, than facts would have sustained;
Howe'er the point she wished was gained;
The time, the place, the whole affair
She knew, and told with serious air.

XIV.

That Laura sprung you may presume;
Her wrappings donned, she left the room,
The stairs descended two-by-two,
Like frightened hare, the hallway through;
The steps she cleared at single bound,
The hostler in a moment found.
His order short, no sooner done,
Than he repaired upon the run;
Her saddle horse he trotted out,
And wheeled him to the block about.
She sprang upon the gentle beast
And turned him heading toward the east;
So trained was he, that as in race,
He shot like arrow from its place.

XV.

She saw the men with arms equipped,
But when she came, like culprit whipped
Each turned as if apart to steal,

And by that means himself conceal.
By name she called them to her side,
Then said: "I beg you drop your pride;
I must be heard, so listen now,
Mark well my words, I make this vow.—
You may not think it lady's part—
But each has asked my hand and heart.
When I have done, my words preserve;
I will not from my answer swerve.

XVI.

The States have joined to try their might,
I scarce know which I deem the right,
   And know not which will win the day;
My brothers for the Union fight,
   My father wars to help the gray.
Go, try in war your power and skill—
You've heard my say, it is my will;—
And when the sanguine war is o'er,
Return, if living, to my door;
To him who wins the highest fame,
I'll give my hand, and take his name.
Mark! each to each must be a friend
Except where battle squadrons bend;
If you shall choose the different sides,
And ever meet where other rides,
Make sure your aim and nerve your arm,
Guard, each himself, against such harm.
If either fall in duty's line
I'll build for him some suited shrine.

XVII.

You 've heard my wish, I 'll wield my power,
It must be done, or from this hour
To him who fails a last adieu;
I leave the rest alone to you."
Her bidding was to them a law,
For love can see no wrong nor flaw.
Each chose as to him seemed the best,
For such had been her last behest.
Since one was son of southern sire,
With all a planter's pride and fire;
Since one had lisped his infant prayer
Upon the Pennsylvania air;
Each choice is known, for this recall,
That early training fashions all.

CUPID AND THE CANNON.

CHAPTER THIRD.

BATTLE.

Shall war's polluted banner ne'er be furled?
Shall crime and tyrants cease but with the world?
Yes! in that generous cause, forever strong,
The patriot's virtue, and the poet's song,
Still, as the tide of ages rolls away,
Shall charm the world, unconscious of decay!
—*Campbell.*

I.

O, foolish man, how can it be
That savage war is waged by thee?
Cans't thou not hear a nation weep,
Ere streams of blood like rivers sweep?
  Proud children of the sunny clime,
Ye must beware the day
  Your armies march to martial time,
Or meet in dread array.
  'T is true, they'll prove a dauntless foe,
Make many a hearthstone bare;
  But of the horror and the woe
On you must fall a double share.
Your strength cannot make good your boasts,

You fight against the Lord of Hosts;
But if you must to conflict fly,
Oh, pity those who live, who die!
For in the wild uncertain game,
To friend and foe alike the same,
King Death will prove the gallant chief;
And Moloch reap the harvest sheaf.

II.

The Southmen rose with mighty power
To join the conflict of the hour,
In countless armies they marched forth
To meet the vanguard of the North;
While Northmen rushed from plain and hill,
And marched to battle with a will.
Two years had passed, the third had come
With cannon roar and battle drum
And struggle fierce and strong;
Hope rose and fell like ocean's tide,
The heroes of our country died
To pay our debt of wrong.
New joy found life in every heart
That loved the Southland and its part,
When Lee marched north with all his train;
But close behind in phalanx broad
The Northmen came to dye the sod
With richest blood of mortal vein.

III.

As if to glory in the scene
So soon to mar the hills of green.

The summer sun rose clear and bright,
While bayonets glistened in the light,
And morning winds a requiem sung,
But battle call more loudly rung,
All to deface the morning sheen.
Yes! noble warrior, hear the call,
　　It is the last thou 'lt ever hear,
It brings thee death, thou needst must fall,
　　And on thy grave no trickling tear.—
It is the cannon's roar that breaks
　　The distant stillness of the morn,
And many a thundering echo wakes,
　　O'er meadows green, and fields of corn.—
The mother hears those echoes roll,
But gone another valiant soul;
She shudders for her soldier son;
His battle o'er, his race well run.—

IV.

The village clock on steeple height,
　　Had struck the noontime hour;
The armies marshaling in their might
　　Were soon to try their power;
For when the clock essayed once more
　　To tell the flight of time,
Its voice was hushed by cannons' roar,
　　That drowned its warning chime.
Ye Northmen, rally undismayed
　　If ye would win the day,
For many a Southman's trusty blade

Is ready for the fray.
Flushed by the triumphs of the past,
    They 've called their troops from near and
        far;
As if the battle were the last,
    And would decide the tide of war.—
Behold the hosts advancing,
    The flower of all the South;
And see the war-horse prancing
    Before the cannon's mouth;
But when the musket speaks
    With voice of death prolonged,
We hear the harrowing shrieks
    Where friend and foe are thronged;
And even the tombs of long gone dead
    Are marked by shot, and torn by shell;
And every grass grown grave is red,
    The awful tale of war to tell.

v.

The loyal winds have ceased to blow,
    For if they waft the stripes and stars,
They know—if winds can ever know—
    They, too, must wave the stars and bars.
The battle smoke hangs in a cloud,
But hark! the thunders long and loud
Have ceased. Then onward to the fray
The Southmen rush, and hope the day
Is won; but well they soon must feel,
That patriot arms are burnished steel;

For, as it were, at but one breath
A thousand thunder peals of death
  Are heard, and victory is the cry.
The Southmen charge, but all too late,
They ne'er will march through loyal state;
  They naught can do but flee or die.
They fought like warriors tried and true,
  Like heroes of a nobler cause;
Against the red, the white, the blue,
  Against the Nation and its laws.
Southward they march—a conquered van—
  With wasted ranks and wearied feet;
Alas for poor misguided man,
  That brothers on the field should meet.

VI.

On every field of battle gory
There can be read a double story,
The one of sorrow, one of glory.
A few triumphant, rise to fame
And leave us an immortal name,
But thousands die, their names unknown,
Oblivion claims them as its own.
See yonder graves so rude and low;
Who sleep within, we cannot know,
A simple slab stands at each head;
Here rest our country's *humble* dead,
And all that 's written on each stone
Is one short word, *unknown, unknown.*

6

VII.

How true the story that they tell,
And yet how false, is known too well:
When that cold form was laid to rest,
With hands scarce folded on his breast;
Without a dirge, without a prayer,
With scarce a sigh or passing care;
At home in some far distant State
He was beloved, his name was great.
O, aged mother, weep no more,
Thy son will come not to thy door,
Thy pride, thy joy has gone above,
No more he'll meet thy smile of love.
Weeks turn to months, and months, to years,
Yet freely flow the mother's tears;
Bent grows her form, her hair, more gray,
But still she seems to hope and pray
That time will bring her darling home;
Until death's feverish dream has come,
And in that dream she seems to see,
And cries, " My darling has come back to me."

VIII.

Perchance a wife, with laughing child,
Thinks of the conflict fierce and wild;
And shudders at the very thought,
Her husband there has cast his lot;
And tears unbidden flow.
Weep, lady, weep! thy life is woe,

Cold is the heart thy hopes enshrine,
A widow's weeds to-day are thine.
Her cradle hymn at night she sings,
And little thinks the echo brings
From battle field, with hollow moan,
The answer back, *unknown, unknown.*

IX.

Perhaps a maiden young and fair
Looks on a lock of raven hair,
Thinks of the time when she will rest
Her head upon that manly breast
And bid her lover welcome there.—
Weep, maiden, weep! thy tears may fall,
Dark is the grave, the cruel pall,
Thy lover cannot hear thy call;
For cold and lifeless is the clay
His comrades rudely place away;
And written on the unhewed stone
That marks his grave, UNKNOWN, UNKNOWN.

X.

How false the story that they tell,
Each vacant hearthstone answers well;
And He who every record keeps
Knows where each fallen hero sleeps.
Shamed be the tear that will not well
For friend and foe who bravely fell;
For though unknown his resting place,
Each shadow seems of him some trace:

His mother, wife, or loved one must
Regret she cannot find his dust,
But echo comes with hollow moan,
And answer brings, UNKNOWN, UNKNOWN.

XI.

Away from the graves where heroes rest,
To where the ghastly wounds are dressed;
Or where, without a murmuring sigh,
The soldiers brave are left to die,
Our transient story bids us hie.—
Two soldiers calmly sleeping lay,
   Wounded, yet brave and young and true.
The one had worn a coat of gray,
   The other wore our country's blue.
In former times they had been foes,
   But now they met as friends;
And friendship oft dispels our woes,
   Or many a solace lends.

XII.

The one who with the Southmen rode
   Was with the troops with which he fought,
But he who other fealty owed
   A prisoner of war was brought;
'T is plain to all who wish to see,
'T was Norman White and Harold Lee.
To most death has a bitter sting,
And yet how often it will bring
   A hope of rest from care,

As many a one, worn with the strife
And sorrow that befall this life,
Sees in the tomb a prospect fair;
But to the young, the true, the brave,
   With life's alluring dream before,
No terror can exceed the grave;
   They shudder at the unknown shore.
To valiant soldier on the field,
   Or weary, sick, or wounded deep
Love proves from death a double shield
   And bids the warrior calmly sleep;
So unto those of whom we write,
There came an angel fair and bright.

XIII.

Harold a queenly sister had,
   Moved by a worthy love she came;
Her presence made the sorrowing glad,
   And Ethel Lee she was by name.
Noble and good and true and kind,
The sick and wounded could but find
She was a faithful friend to all;
Through weary day, through half the night,
Always cheerful, ever bright,
She toiled within the ward's dark wall.
Her tender love and watchful care
   Soon called her brother back to life;
When, with a sister's parting prayer,
   He turned once more to fields of strife.

XIV.

Before he left, he sought the place
Where Norman slumbering lay,
And to his sister gently said,
"I see death gathering in his face;
Until he goes I beg you stay;
And when he is numbered with the dead
    Choose out for him some little bower,
And have him kindly laid to rest;
    Soothe as you can his dying hour;
By Heaven above we will be blessed—
I go to war, and he, to rest.
    Poor Norman, 'tis the soldier's fate
For one to win, and one to loose;
    But life's best prize is not so great,
If one its all could choose.
    Now, dearest sister, fare ye well!
A parting kiss and then I leave;
    The fates of war are hard to tell,
But o'er our lot we should not grieve;
And whether good or ill befall,
I trust I'll answer duty's call;
Farewell! dear sister, fare ye well!"
The one must sleep while others weep,
    His lamp of life is burning low;
But love and care, that matchless pair,
    Exert a power that none can know.

CUPID AND THE CANNON.

CHAPTER FOURTH.

THE ESCAPE.

And yet he has another monument, an eternal monument erected by the hand of God.
—Noble L. Prentis.

I.

The sun had set behind a cloud
From which the thunders echoed loud;
The moon, in haste to hide away,
Had followed close the orb of day;
Swift angry clouds blew through the sky;
The wind alternate low and high,
Sometimes with soft and hollow moan
And then with fierce and angry tone,
Blew o'er Virginia's hills afar,
Where rolled the billowy tide of war.
The soldier dreamed of conflict wild,
Or else of wife and laughing child,
Or of the home of youthful years,
And of a mother's prayers and tears.
The sentry trod his lonely beat,
Not knowing whom or what he'd meet,

Or but some figure in the gloom
Had marked him for the soldier's tomb.
Dark loomed the prison walls aloft,
Unless the night all shadows scoffed.

II.

Long had it been the home or den
Of creatures vile, but not of men;
There had the bat oft flown by night,
The owl secreted from the light;
Howe'er the owl and bat no more
Sought refuge in its lamplit door,
For in those walls so old and gray,
There many a wounded soldier lay;
While nurses, moving here and there,
Bestowed, as best they could, their care:—
To one a cup of water given,
To one, a word of death and heaven;
Another, ere he go, must leave
    A word of love, a last sad token,
And—"Tell the dear ones not to grieve,
    But meet me where no ties are broken.
This picture, which I beg you save,
    Long have I carried next my heart;
It seemed to make me doubly brave,
    I'll kiss it once "—a sudden start,
His hand lies powerless on his breast,
    The picture fallen at his side;
Poor soldier! he has gone to rest,
    And left a lonely, weeping bride.

III.

Hard to the east a forest stood,
It was an ancient, stately wood;
So dense, the sun on summer noon
Shone as some pale, some recent moon.
Within that forest shade so dark,
Without a starlight's glimmering spark,
And where the whip-poor-will's love notes
Were chanted by a dozen throats,
A maiden brave and young and fair,
As if inured to toil and care,
Along a narrow pathway sped,
Like one whose mind is filled with dread.
Beside her walked a noble steed
   As ever saddled for the race;
She hastened on; nor seemed to heed,
   The horse was wild, and proud his pace,
Until she reached a little mound
That stood with scattered shrubs around,
Just where a fallen oak tree lay;
Then stopped, and listening, seemed to say.—

IV.

"My throbbing heart beats fast perforce,
Ay, well it may! at this my course;
But 'all in love and war is fair,'
An ancient saying doth declare;
Naught else but war with its stern laws
Could ever prove sufficient cause

That lady, child of care and wealth,
Should darkness choose, and come by stealth
To meet in this secluded spot
Some new-found friend, yet such I ought.
I saved him from the grave's stern hold,
But not to die in prison fold;
Although his cause my brothers hate,
I'll save him from so sad a fate.

v.

"Yes, he is brave and kind and true,
Of nobler men there are but few;
And e'en perhaps our cause is worse;
Slavery, to earth has been a curse,
And it the blight that makes our land
To flow with blood by brother's hand.
I bribed the guard with glittering gold—
Honor for pelf is often sold—
That guard ere this he must have passed—
I hear him come, he's safe at last!"
'T was thus the loyal Norman White,
Upon that dark and stormy night
Escaped the troops that wore the gray,
And started on his unknown way
Toward where the Union army lay.
Few parting words by them were spoken,
Of love there was not sign or token;
But Ethel quickly left the place,
And toward the Southland turned her face;
While he to northward bent his course,
Mounted upon that noble horse.

VI.

The night was dark, the wind was fierce,
While not a star the clouds could pierce;
Unknown the way through which to ride,
With deadly foes on either side;
Full ninety miles through wood and brake,
With liberty or life the stake,
His way with him let us betake.
True to his course hour after hour,
His horse appeared to gather power,
Though hills behind him seemed to fly
Like clouds across the stormy sky;
Until at last his way was lost
Long ere he reached our country's host.
Through trackless wood, dark, dark, and deep,
Sick, tired, hungry, needing sleep,
His course he wound as best he could,
But found no way from out the wood,
Until the dawning of the day,
When all too late he found his way.

VII.

His horse to dark ravine he led
Where all was silent as the dead,
Save now and then a flitting breeze
That rustled through the o'erhanging trees.
What now to do he did not know,
On every hand no doubt a foe;
If friend in reach, he knew not where,

To search for such he did not dare.
Some victuals he had brought along,
For he was neither well nor strong;
A breakfast and an hour of rest
Renewed the courage in his breast;
When, leaving horse in deepest shade,
Over the hills his way he made
Until a cabin he espied
Just at the forest's northern side.
An hour he watched, or even more,
When a dark form came from the door;
A man, as black as is the smoke
That pours from pit of burning coke.
Into the wood straightway he came,
It matters not his age or name.
From thence he carried all his wood,
A living got as best he could.
A moment Norman stopped to think;
He stood as if on chasm's brink,
And might escape without a blow
Or might be hurled to depths below;
Then boldly walked to where the black
Stood like a statue in his track.
The man of color seemed to fear,
He trembled as a captured deer
Until assured a friend addressed,
And then he spoke with hearty zest:

VIII.

" Oh how I loves old Massa Abe!
For he 's de one what freed the slabe;
And how I wish his troops would come,
I dreams at night I hears de drum.
If you be one dat wore de blue,
Why, dis de child to help you through.
I 'll gib you what you wants to eat,
Some bread of corn, we hab no meat,
And feed your hoss, as well as you;
Don't be afraid but I 'll be true.
I 'll hide you where you 's safe and sound
As if you 's buried in de ground;
And call you when de dark comes forth,
And start you on the road up north."

IX.

Within a cave in mountain breast
The soldier took his sleep and rest;
To speed the lonely hours along,
Among the rest he hummed this song:

> I love my native country,
>   With mountains broad and steep;
> I love her boundless prairies,
>   With rivers wide and deep,
>   That
> Rolling, rolling, rolling
>   Forever toward the sea,
>
>   Go
> Laughing, singing, laughing,
>   So happy and so free.

I love her eastern hillsides,
   Where rests ancestral dust;
And know that with our fathers,
   Soon all the living must
        Be
Sleeping, calmly sleeping,
   The young, the fair, the strong,
        While
Weeping, laughing, weeping,
   The world will roll along.

I love our starry banner,
   The people's hope and pride;
To found and save our country
   Our fathers bled and died.
        With
Loving, toiling, dying,
   This human lot must be;
        But
Deathless as the mountains,
   The banner of the free.

x.

Norman, his horse well fed and groomed,
At night his perilous way resumed.
The night was dark as was the last,
The wind still blew in fitful blast;
The horse leaped nobly to his task,
His rider need not spur nor ask.
As if he knew his master's need,
Hour after hour he kept his speed,
Save tightened reign reserved his strength;
His rider knew the way had length
And let him keep but moderate pace.
But hark! the foe have given chase,

A score of horsemen clad in gray,
In headlong gait are on the way.
They 're mounted well, their horses strong,
Nor has their way to-night been long.
A messenger, they think he rides;
To capture such each foeman prides;
Then wildly in pursuit they spring,
Each horse seems swift as bird on wing;
But his a steed both strong and fleet,
Used to the race and sure of feet,
Inured to Southern summer heat.

XI.

A pale light in the eastern sky
Proclaims the dawn of day is nigh;
Then harder to the chase they bend,
For soon they know the race must end;
And he, as well, now slacks the rein
And lets his horse each strong nerve strain.
Swift as a comet through the skies,
Upon its fiery pinion flies.
Still bounds his steed with hearty will
Across each valley and over each hill;
Yet close they come, and closer after,
He hears their oaths, he hears their laughter,
While many a leaden ball flies 'round,
Yet harmless falls upon the ground.

XII.

Steep is the hill and rough the road,
The horse grows weary with his load;

His breath is coming thick and fast,
But little longer can he last.
At length the race came to an end,
For, o'er the hilltop, 'round the bend
A hundred horsemen came to view,
Each clad in soldier's coat of blue.
A minute's chase and all was changed,
Those who pursued, in columns ranged,
Rode slowly, but in sullen mood,
Toward where a Union prison stood;
While Norman looked on stripes and stars
And thought of Rebel stars and bars.
He thanked the Fates that he no more
Beheld them fly o'er prison door;
And vowed his country still to serve,
If God his life so long preserve,
Until the stars and stripes should stand
The emblem of a peaceful land;
Then took his needed food and rest,
Nor woke till sun was in the west.

CUPID AND THE CANNON.

CHAPTER FIFTH.

THE SPY.

And green forever be the groves,
    And bright the flowery sod,
Where first the child's glad spirit loves
    Its country and its God.

                          —*Mrs. Hemans.*

I.

The chieftain of the Union force
    Sat in his tent, with furrowed brow;
He pondered long upon his course,
    Just what to do, and when, and how.
Upon his knee a war-map lay,
    From which he sought a plan to form;
He hoped to move the coming day—
    The heavens presaged an early storm.
The other leaders sat around;
    They counseled long, some paced the tent,
Some idly sat upon the ground,
    Some o'er the map of war were bent.
They more must learn about the foe,
    About his arms, and of his planning:

Among his ranks a spy must go,
  The country and his numbers scanning.
They all concurred that they must send
  A man in every place unyielding,
Whom nothing from his path could bend,
  And yet himself most wisely shielding.
He must be skillful, all agreed,
  As shrewd as wolf in ancient fable;
Of danger take but little heed,
  To travel fast and far be able.

II.

The scouts and spies have been passed by,
  The bards sing not their valorous deeds;
'T is just as brave to dare to die
  Alone, as where the phalanx leads.
The Wilderness had just been fought,
  The eagle's wings were badly torn;
No pomp—the charge—the deadly shot,
  And back the Union lines were borne.
When our proud eagle finds his wings
  Are likely to be torn apart,
He from his rocky eyrie springs,
  And sinks his talons to the heart.

III.

"I'll bring your man," an aid replied,
  "Just wait a moment if you please."
He soon returned, and by his side
  A youth who walked with athlete's ease.

The ancient sculptors never dreamed
  Of human form with all his grace;
With stately brow, he would have seemed
  To them as of a noble race.
Columbia's sons and daughters are
  Fit models for the sculptor's art;
Excelling other lands by far
  In grace of form, of mind, of heart.

IV.

A son of Erin trod along,
  He asked and begged for work in vain;
His spirits he would cheer with song,
  Some soft pathetic Irish strain;
Meet strangers, and his eyes would dim,
  As, sighing for his native shore,
He would lament the fate of him
  Who, hungry, begged from door to door.
One hand hung loosely at his side,
  Devoid of shape, it scarcely moved;
Without success he daily tried,
  His wrinkled hand such hindrance proved.
He often begged the negroes' care;
  Yet leaving, he would find—by chance—
Some bill to pay thrice o'er his fare;
  And watched them as their eyes would
    dance.

V.

As by a log one night he slept,
  With sudden starting he awoke,

And doubtless closer to it crept,
    As some one near his refuge spoke.
There came and sat upon the log
    Three men, and to themselves rehearsing—
The moon was hid with heavy fog—
    He heard them tell with useless cursing,
How they had shot a spy that day,
    And one had hung the night before;
That every doubtful man must die,
    To this their leader loudly swore.
They freely talked, and told their strength,
    At least what they supposed to be;
Conjectured plans, until at length
    They moved away—and so did he.

VI.

"Halt!" broke the stillness of the night;
    He stopped and stood as if of stone;
Beyond a brook he saw a light,
    A smouldering fire, and one alone.
A rifle blazed, a ball came singing,
    He heard it whistling through the wood;
He, like a shadow swiftly springing
    Behind a tree, in silence stood.
For farther move he calmly waited,
    But little more was heard;
Except the private was berated
    For firing at a bird.
The officers will sometimes blame
    When praise is due the picket:

He waited long, but no one came—
   It was a thorny thicket.

VII.

Sly as the wary panther steals
   So stole he from his hiding;
For carelessness he doubtless feels
   A pricking conscience chiding.
Howe'er it be, he stole around,
   Heeding the sentry's warning;
A scouter's camp was all he found;
   He left it ere the morning.
For miles the woodland stretched before,
   Deep in its midst a narrow clearing;
He heard the distant river roar,
   But human voice broke on his hearing.
From hill to hill the echo rung,
And this the song a negro sung:

SONG.

When I reach de great hereafter,
   And am free from earthly wrong,
I 'll not weep, but go with laughter
   To increase de heavenly throng.

Hark! I hear de angels calling, calling,
   Calling from de odder shore;
Hark! I hear der footsteps falling, falling,
   Falling on my cabin floor.

Life to me is bery dreary,
   Sorrows more dan heart can bear;
So my soul is growing weary
   To ascend de golden stair.

Hark! I think I hear dem singing, singing,
  Singing some angelic lay;
Dere my voice will soon be ringing, ringing,
  Ringing, for I 's gwine that way.

All my life is full of trouble,
  Man to man is bery bad;
When de Lord shall break dis bubble,
  I 'll be truly, truly glad.

Hark! new voices now are waking, waking,
  Waking in de chorus loud;
See! de light of day is breaking, breaking,
  Breaking through de heaby cloud.

VIII.

The song was done, its cadence lost
  Along the Rappahannock's shore;
The trees with passing gusts were tossed,
  The wild birds sang—and nothing more.
The listener wondering sat, and gazed
  Across the fields, strange fears encroaching,
Until by chance his eyes he raised
  And saw a squad of horse approaching.
Dismounting, each prepared to eat,
  For long and hard the band had ridden;
The leader first approached the seat
  Where he had thought himself well hidden.

IX.

The portly captain asked his name,
  And why, alone, he sat there thinking.
" Faith! Patrick Murphy is the same,
  And sure, I would be afther drinking.

Sir, I 'm hungry as you pl'ase,
  And b'astly tired of this trampin';
While you are ridin' at your 'ase,
  Or loafin' round the place of campin';
And could you walk a bit sir, pl'ase?
  And then I would be afther ridin';
But first, I 'll go and ate with ye's,
  Two gintlemen the m'al dividin'."

x.

The soldiers smiled to hear him sigh
  For Erin, gem of all the ocean;
When one pronounced the man a spy,
  And thereby caused a slight commotion.
They led some horses; how procured
  It matters not, for human feeling
Is much the same we are assured,
  And taking is not always stealing.
The horses done with their foray—
  No extra time was left for feeding—
They, mounting, with him rode away,
  Mazeppa-like the streams unheeding.

xi.

Adown the river's northeast bank
  They rode, but never stopped for pillage;
And nothing ate, and nothing drank,
  Until they reached a little village.
The hamlet was a rendezvous
  For officers half sick or wounded;

Of prisoners there were a few,
  And all the place with guards surrounded.
A thorough search revealed no proof,
  No cause for Patrick's condemnation;
And threats of hanging to the roof
  Increased his cry of lamentation.

XII.

They bound him firmly to a wall,
  Then left him to his own reflections.
It was a low-built, straggling hall
  With sheds built 'round in all directions;
For hospital at present kept,
  One wing some nurses occupying;
Now all was still, the weary slept,
  There was no wail, no voice of crying.
Those rugged walls, that floor of stone
  Had sometimes heard the captive's moan,
Had wakened to the dying groan;
  But now to him 't was left alone.

XIII.

Two nurses carried supper 'round,
  One saw his eyes and gave a start,
She checked herself, but with a bound
  She left the room like frightened hart.
Just where the dark and daylight meet
  That nurse returned, alone was she;
She walked like sprite, with noiseless feet,
  A fairer none could wish to see.

A minute only she remained,
  No matter what their conversation;
His old time spirits he regained,
  While she resumed her occupation.

XIV.

With brogue to suit, now grave, now gay,
He softly sung this humble lay,
To while the weary hours away:

SONG.

A poor roving child of the Emerald Isle,
  I am thinking to-day of thy surf-beaten shore,
Of a mother's caress, and a fond sister's smile,
  And a cabin that stands with a vine by the door.

She is fair as a flower, as the queen of the bower
  Are the locks on her rosy cheeks curling;
She is as sweet as the May, and whatever you say,
  She is worth half a million of sterling.

A cabin of earth with a roof formed of straw
  Is the home of the lass, my pride and my joy;
I think of her standing, the last that I saw,
  And the kiss that she threw to her own Irish boy.

I will work night and day for my sweet bonnie girl,
  I will build us a home in America free;
She is bright as a rose, and—that sly little curl—
  How I sigh for my lass to come over the sea !

XV.

With tune unchanged he sung a song
That mourned his country and her wrong:

Our grandsires, the Celts, were once happy and brave,
  But now o'er their tombs the fell Saxon lord gloats;

Our sires owned the island from center to wave,
    But the hand of the tyrant is firm on our throats.

No happier land ever sprung from His hand,
    From the hand of the bountiful Master;
By nature 't is blessed, but by tyrants oppressed;
    I must weep at my country's disaster.

We work all the day for a morsel of bread,
    And the place where we sleep is a bundle of straw.
The landlord will tear down the roof from o'er head,
    And England will call it a merciful law.

O England, your wrongs will at last be repaid,
    The God of the nations will balance His own;
Unless you repay, by your crimes over weighed,
    The waves of His wrath will encircle your throne.

XVI.

When sleep had settled o'er the place,
    Another came, with step like thief;
He left no track, not any trace,
    Though black as Congo's native chief.
The guards next morning came around,
    But lo! the prisoner had fled;
They left him there securely bound,
    But found the naked walls instead.
An all day search no trace revealed,
    Though numbers were in it concerned;
On every road, across each field,
    But bootless all at last returned.

XVII.

Next evening, as the Union ranks
    Had pitched their camp, to rest the night,

And pickets guarded well the flanks,
  Before, behind, to left, to right,
There came a vagrant Irish tramp,
Who sought admittance to the camp.
How he secured the envied boon
Will be revealed, but not too soon.

CUPID AND THE CANNON.

CHAPTER SIXTH.

PEACE.

" Lo! peace on earth! Lo! flock and fold,
Lo! rich abundance, far increase,
   And valleys clad in sheen of gold,
     Oh, rise and sing the song of peace!
   For Theseus roams the land no more,
   And Janus rests with rusted door."
              —C. H. Miller.

I.

Though bullet wound and sabre scar
Are but the natural fruit of war;
Though scenes, as stormy midnight black,
Must follow in the army's track,
A tale of war were half untold
That only praised the chieftain bold.
The humble private of the ranks
Deserves as much a nation's thanks
As laureled chieftain ever earns;
His bosom with true fervor burns,
He nobly to his duty turns;
And live or die it is the same,
His is the real hero's fame.

No trump of praise sounds in his ears,
He hears no wild huzzas of cheers,
He sees a widow's weeds and tears;
An orphan's wail his only fears.
For him should Honor's trumpet bay,
For him be sung the deathless lay.

II.

O woman, angel from above,
Boundless as space thy heavenly love,
However broad this space may be;
A more than kind and generous Heaven
To earth no other gift has given
That can at all compare with thee.
They say, as vine entwines the oak,
Nor fears the woodman's deadly stroke,
So thou to man art clinging found
Wherever peace and love abound.
Woman, when joy from thee has flown,
Thou hast a courage of thy own,
A strength that man can never know,
Nor fails till death has laid thee low.
A hundred names we might recall
And sing the praises of them all;
But time forbids, one answers well,
An angel now, poor Mary Bell!

III.

Nor happier home to mortals lent,
Than that in which thy youth was spent;

Thy years were free from toil and strife,
Nor early cares weighed down thy life
Till fratricidal war had burst
Upon our land; among the first
Thy brothers from the ramparts hurled
The shots that woke a wondering world.
The call for nurses quickly came,
Among the first thou wrote'st thy name,
And bravely did thy duty do,
To every call and beckon true.
Months changed to years, and war's dread tide
Rolled o'er the land from side to side;
But not the fever's wasting blight,
Nor even battle cannons' might,
Could drive thee for an hour apart
From where kind Mercy swayed thy heart.

IV.

Thy eyes grew dim, thy cheeks grew pale,
Thy wonted strength began to fail;
Physicians said to take thy rest,
But duties all around thee pressed;
Thy tender heart with pity burned,
And nature's call to rest was spurned
Until there came the final word
That soon or late, all will have heard.
A nation's thanks that tell of love
Are heard the din of war above;
And eyes grow dim with tears that tell

The praise of thee, poor Mary Bell:
The winds are sighing, " Fare thee well."

v.

At last 't is done! the sounds of war
    Sink in a dying strain;
Their last dread thunders from afar
    Sound o'er each hill and plain.
Fainter, and still more faint they grow,
    Until their lingering echo dies;
They leave a land plunged deep in woe,
    While clouds are rolling through the skies.
Peace! at the word how every heart
    Bounds with a thrill of untold joy!
And yet the tears unbidden start,
    For many a mother mourns her boy.
The widows weep for husbands slain;
    Ten thousand sisters sadly mourn,
For brothers sleep on battie plain,
    And home is of its loved one's shorn;
While many a luckless orphan cries,
And all the land is filled with sighs.

VI.

The marshaled hosts with stars and bars,
    Have passed their swords to victor's hand;
The eagle, from among the stars,
    Looks on a reunited land.
The conquered Southman casts away
    The emblem he so bravely followed;

While loyal hands our flag array,
    By brothers' blood thrice doubly hallowed.
Now slowly toward his ruined home
    His weary steps the vanquished turns;
But through his mind what torrents come,
    What anguish in his bosom burns,
As he looks o'er his wasted state,
    Beholds the ruin war has wrought,
Thinks of the Southland's promise great,
    And of her present lowly lot.

VII.

Northward toward home the victor goes,
    Some song of youth or childhood humming;
For he has triumphed o'er his foes,
    And knows the dear ones wait his coming;
But, ah! how many wait in vain
    To hear a footstep at the door;
A step that ne'er will sound again,
    But softly treads the silent shore.
That limping walk, that empty sleeve,
    Each helps to tell a tale of sorrow;
Though most about their own must grieve,
    Nor need a cause of tears to borrow.
In money, men can count the cost
    That war brings on a nation;
But when we think of young lives lost,
    And hear the lamentation;

And when we think of human blood,
   Adown like torrents flowing,
With aching hearts we see the flood,
   The price there is no knowing.

VIII.

The planter's mansion rose to view
Beneath the evening skies of blue;
Little of change the war had brought,
For that had been a peaceful spot.
Although the blacks were slaves no more,
A few toiled 'round the mansion door;
Hardship and time had made their mark
Upon the planter's visage dark;
The wrinkles written on his face
Proclaimed that time had kept its pace.
Laura, no more a giddy child
With thoughtless ways and laughter wild,
Had grown to woman's perfect sphere;
Her voice was music to the ear,
And told a heart of real worth,
The richest treasure of the earth.

IX.

The foolish ways of youthful years
Had brought of late a weight of fears;
A sound of horsemen on the road,
Or neighbors passing with a load,
Would make her start with quickened breath,
Like one in fear of harm or death.

She knew the yearnings of her heart,
  At last she felt the growing flame;
For this she feared, each sudden start
  Recalled her childish freak with shame.
At thoughts of one, the tender strings
That wake the songs of love were strung;
The other, o'er her shadows flung,
And bore her hopes on raven's wings.

X.

One evening late in 'sixty-four,
  She sat and wondered how it 't would be,
When the post-boy, calling at the door,
  A letter left that set her free.
The letter, couched in language kind,
Plainly revealed an altered mind;
Releasing her, it asked the same
For him who wrote—and bore the blame.
More welcome words, however laden,
Were seldom penned by man to maiden;
Her laughter took the joyous ring
  That it had had in days of old,
While long neglected songs she 'd sing,
  The raptures of her heart that told.

XI.

On sinful mortals here below
  A drop of heavenly bliss may fall;
There is a joy for every woe,
  Though earthly pleasures oft seem small.

If memory to life is true—
    It seldom fails in duty—
There oft transpires our country through
    A scene of wondrous beauty.
We 're led upon this theme to say
    There should not then be peeping;
'T is better from the world away,
    Or else when it is sleeping.
No arm can render any aid
    To those who are the nearest;
'T is when a lover wooes the maid,
    Of earth he deems the dearest,
The golden rule will here apply,
    So pass ye with averted eye.

XII.

Swiftly the summer days had glided,
    Until their race was over;
The green with brown had been divided
    In fields of corn and clover.
When evening drew her heavy curtain,
    And wrapped the mansion in,
A gayer home, we feel full certain,
    Has seldom ever been.
From cellar to the topmost rafter,
    Of that old mansion hall,
Resounded joyous shouts of laughter
    That shook the very wall;
The lights that from the window shone

Lit up the yards and groves surrounding—
The colored lights so freely thrown,
  With red and white and blue abounding;
The wedding bells pealed out that night
  A double chime, both strong and free:
Now Ethel Lee is Mrs. White,
  And Laura Blair is Mrs. Lee.

XIII.

The prisoner, the tramp so lame,
The Union spy, are all the same.
It must be plain to all who read—
Perhaps their lot was never worse—
So plain, there is but little need
To say that Ethel was the nurse.
The horse, she brought for him to ride,
She looked upon with Arab's pride;
And he, the favorite horse who rode,
Of life bears more than half her load.
She taunts her brother with his lack
  Of power to pierce the tramp's disguise;
But he, the captain, answers back
  With merry twinkle in his eyes,
He knew him well, but knew her heart,
And spared him for his sister's part.

XIV.

The faithful negro who unbound
  The Irish spy and helped him flee,
Has given the horse a grass-grown mound

And keeps it from all brambles free.
Near where the "Massa's" dwelling stands,
   Back in a shaded quietnook
He lives, and tills their fruitful lands;
   You'll see his cottage if you look.
He and his wife in comfort dwell,
   A model pair, and more than that
'T is useless here of them to tell,
   Except their boy is christened Pat.

XV.

The sun of May is brightly shining,
   The groves with merry song birds ring;
No sound of sorrow or repining
   The winds across the praires bring.
Two orchards blooming o'er the way,
   Two houses standing near together;
A happy place on every day,
   A cheerful scene in dullest weather.
Hard by, a city of the plain,
   A proud young city of the west
Surrounded with great fields of grain,
   'T is here they dwell by fortune blessed.
Honor may never cross their hearth,
   At best it is an empty name;
A happy home is heaven on earth,
   A neighbor's praise is more than fame.
And such, at least, has been the meed
   Of those whose life these pages tell.

Bliss to their homes, from trouble freed,
  Peace to our land, to them, farewell.

*   *   *   *   *   *   *   *

Northman and Southman, my tale is told,
Of loving maid, of warrior bold,
Of some whose hearts have long been cold.
The war, with all its scenes of wrong,
Is suited theme for poet's song
If he but plays the patriot's part,
Nor seeks to wound with poisoned dart;
But right is right, and wrong is crime,
On history's page, in idle rhyme.
To me, the battle call and cheers
Are memories of childhood's years;
Or truer still, to me they seem
The creatures of some horrid dream;
But yet, to many a vacant home,
Like some gaunt skeleton they come.
All now is passed, forget! forgive,
The dead cannot, but those who live
Can teach that war and all its crimes
Are relics of barbaric times,
And help to ring the sacred chimes,
That shall resound through every glen
Of "peace on earth, good will toward men!"

THE LIGHTNING AND THE BOOK AGENT.

AFTER THE MANNER OF THE LEGENDS.

One morning in winter the lightning went out
  To travel awhile on the road;
As the day wore away, it went rambling about
  Till it met a man bearing a load.

The lightning was rude, and approaching, it
    spoke
  In a way that was shocking, indeed;
It proposed that they fight—though it meant
    but to joke—
  The man listened, and paid it good heed.

"I am poor," said the man, "and most truly I
    fear
  That my wife and my children will die
If I'm taken away;" and a great rolling tear
  Could be seen in the poor farmer's eye.

A carriage drove up; when the lightning
    began,
  And it talked to the driver the same;
But it this time had met with a different man,
  And this is the answer that came.

"I am happy to meet you, my dear worthy
    friend,

118 A KNIGHTLY SHIELD.

And I pray you will listen to me,
An ear of attention I trust you will lend,
  While I tell of V. A. B. & C."

The lightning was angry and struck him a
    blow,
But rebounded a rod from his cheek;
The agent drove on, and the farmer lay low,
  While the lightning was crippled and weak.

I have given the reason, that all winter through
  The lightning is peaceful and still;
As it told me the tale I repeat it to you,
  For the agent then roams at his will.

A KNIGHTLY SHIELD.

At Eutaw Springs, in 'eighty-one,
The British were compelled to run;
Their hold within the South was done.

A soldier brave and lithe and strong,
Who fought against a tyrant's wrong,
Pursued the foe almost too long.

Although he followed all alone,
Against them all he held his own,
Like monarch on his gilded throne.

He grasped a Briton by the coat;
He even took him by the throat,
Roughly as farmer would a shoat.

The Yankee seized the Briton's sword
And hastened back, his comrades towards,
At which his angry captive roared.

He cried aloud with all his might:
"I'd have you know, you ruthless wight,
I am a lordly British knight.

"Sir Henry Barry is my name,
Perhaps you may have heard the same,
To treat me thus is deadly shame."

"Enough, enough!" his captor cried,
"To match with you I long have tried,
There is a bounty on your hide."

He kept the Briton as a shield,
Retreating swiftly from the field;
His prowess made Sir Henry yield.

A knightly buckler, I confess,
Was never used with much success;
But Manning did it, none the less.

Peace to the patriot's lowly tomb
Who helped dispel our country's gloom;
May grasses grow and lilies bloom.

POOR OLD DASH.

There are places on earth that are dear to each
    one,
By the brook where we played when the school
    day was done,
In the orchard where grew the best fruit ever
    grown,
And the blossoms were brightest that ever have
    blown.

There's a spot in the meadow just over the way,
From the home of my childhood where fancy
    will stray,
I can yet see the flowers as they lovingly wave,
O'er the place where in boyhood I helped make
    a grave.

Not the grave of a human, though sweet be
    each rest,
In the North, or the South, or the unbounded
    West;
But the love of the dead, though his race was
    another,
Proved so true that I mourned at his death as
    a brother.

Poor old Dash was a dog, and my age was
    just five,

When they brought him, a puppy, the cutest
  alive.
How my heart gave a bound! Oh, the rapture
  and joy,
That this world can afford to an innocent boy!

I recall with a sigh—and great tears I have
  shed—
How, in anger, I struck the poor dog on the
  head;
But before half an hour he returned with a
  bound
And he saved me from death, or at least from
  a wound.

Though he fought against odds, he was true
  to his trust,
For his blood flowed so freely it reddened the
  dust;
Yet he failed not a moment, but fought undismayed,
Till the sound of the strife called a neighbor
  to aid.

All ye children who read, if ye learn to be good
To the beast that ye meet and the bird of the
  wood;
If ye learn to be gentle and kind in your play,
It will bring its reward ere the close of the day.

IN A LADY'S ALBUM.

If you ask me what most pleasant
    Is man's gift on earth below,
I must answer for the present,
    As for that I scarcely know;
But if ladies all were missing
I should move to banish kissing.

FOUR STEPS DOWNWARD.

This story is told in a book of old,
    In a book of the ancient times;
How the earth became polluted with shame,
    And the heir of its countless crimes.

How man at first with the bowl was cursed,
    With the cup of the sparkling wine;
For he did not know of the human woe
    That was hid where the red drops shine.

The tempter appeared, and, as nothing was
      feared,
    A most willing subject was found;
Man took but one draught, then turning, he
      laughed,
    And a peacock, he strutted around.

He once again drank, and the proud bird sank,
    And a monkey was plain to see;
He imbibed once more, and with deafening
    roar
A ferocious lion was he.

Once more at the grog, and a filthy hog
    Lay wallowing in the street.—
Such fables recall the stages that all
    Who "tarry" too long must meet.

O people, awake and the fetters break,
    The shackles that are so strong;
For drink is the source, and a mighty force
    In the march of earthly wrong.

Dark streams of woe from this fountain flow;
    And till men can grow more bold,
The prison wall, so grim and so tall,
    Will be filled as full as 't will hold.

For "liberty's sake," it is foolish to break
    The hearts of the young and the fair;
For they are but weak, and the stronger should
    seek
The weight of the burden to bear.

All praise to our land, and palsied the hand
    That a jot from its honor would sever;
But a burning shame will rest on our name
    Till the dramshop is banished forever.

THE ROVER.

Though far from native hills to roam,
His heart turns back as child's toward home;
He sees the cottage where of late
In childish glee around the gate
He played at ball or turtle-dove,
Singing some childish lay of love;
And little thinking that the years
Would come too fast with hopes and fears;
And that the grave so soon would call
Some loved ones to its silent wall.

How fast Time writes his fatal brand
On every human brow and hand;
But hills and river are the same,
They alter not in form or name,
To them the flight of years is strange,
They, laughing, mock Time's wasting change.
The birds will sing the same sweet song,
    The brooklet ripple as before,
When his young spirit now so strong
    Shall seek that distant shore.
The river, on whose banks he played
    When truant from the master's care,
Will laugh with those who then have strayed,
    To seek for pleasure there.

Sing, river, as thou wind'st thy way,
   Mid'st pine-girt hills down toward the sea,
While he, a wanderer far astray
   In distant clime, shall think of thee.
So fast has flowed time's ceaseless flood
   It seems to him but yestermorn,
Since first upon thy banks he stood
   And heard the boatman sound his horn.
The boats now deemed so old and slow,
   No more upon thy waters ride;
Instead, the locomotives go
   Fast thundering up each side.

At thoughts of thee rise hopes and fears,
His mind reverts to childhood's years,
Thinks of its joys, forgets its tears.
Who would not give half that he own,
E'en were it wealth or fame or throne,
For but one hour of careless joy,
To be an idle, thoughtless boy;
To have a mother smooth his hair
With only a mother's love and care;
Oh, could he turn the tide of years!
For childhood's bliss he'd take its tears.

No wives and daughters o'er the main
   Have hearts as brave, as kind, as true;
No homes where peace and plenty reign,
   As in our own broad land they do.
The human heart is wondrous strange,

We love the place we dwell on earth;
The groves through which we joy to range,
    Nor less, the place that gave us birth.
Let those who wish in cities dwell;
    His own green prairies free and wild,
Fair Kansas with her restless winds
    Is dearer to her rugged child.

Where'er through all the land we roam
    The same domestic joys are seen;
The happiest place of all is home,
    From Croix to San Joaquin.—
The theme must change—but then—
Home is a loftier theme by far
Than are the surging scenes of war,
Home and the schools can make or mar
The destinies of men.

The youth, accustomed to the hills
    And mighty forests' sombre shades,
Whose life has passed beside the rills
    That murmur through his native glades,
At first feels lonely at the view,
    Sees nothing in our azure sky;
No damsel fair with eyes of blue
    Dwells in his heart and swells the sigh.
He mourns his native hills and mountains,
The forests and their purling fountains.

His vision o'er, his day dream fails,
    The cares of busy life engage;

The welcome task he gladly hails,
    Toil smooths the pathway down to age.
The country of his birth behind;
    Where once the Montezumas ruled
He wends his way, his heart resigned,
    To Arab's life fast being schooled.
Great mountains look on verdant vales
    Where tropic fruits profusely grow;
The snow-capped peaks, like fairy tales,
    Shine where the groves of orange blow.

Queretaro attracts his view,
    'T was there that Maximilian fell;
A freeman's tears are not *his* due,
    When tyrants fall it is as well.
The brave young prince had better bleed
    Than live to found a robber's throne;
He only met a fitting meed;
    Our continent is freedom's own.
Be as it may, the passer by
    That sheds a tear upon the spot
May not the freeman's faith belie,
    Perhaps he mourns Carlotta's lot.

The rambler's steps I may not trace,
    For time is on the wing to-night;
He saw full many a novel place,
    In vintage vale, on mountain height.
What there he heard and what he learned
    Is theme for tale or studied lay;

But home his footsteps he has turned,
  Resolved, ere long to farther stray.
When on his native soil he trod
  His heart leaped with a sudden bound,
Renewed his faith in man and God,
  As on the scene he looked around.
In tones unskilled, with hearty will
This song awoke the neighboring hill.

SONG.

Where'er the freeman's footsteps roam
  The cottage home of childhood
Appears above the stately dome,
  And streets are turned to wildwood.

Let others boast of marshaled host,
  Columbia's homes and schools
Will train the hand to bless the land
  Where smiling plenty rules.

O God of nations, guide the State,
  Our banner safely shielding;
Raise up a people strong and great,
  To Thee their homage yielding.

THREE PICTURES.

If the painter had power from the rainbow to
    gather
  The colors that girdle the skies;
I should order three pictures—in one I should
    rather—
  Alike in their form and their size.

The first would be wheat-field and wood land,
    and mild would
  Be the colors and tinting of all;
It would be of a farm, just a picture of
    childhood,
  Over which not a shadow must fall.

In the valley below the old school-house
    appearing,
  And the teacher still there in the door,
With the smile of his kindness the picture en-
    dearing
  To the boy he once stood on the floor.

In the next would be manhood—but see how it
    rushes!
  O painter, make haste or you fail;
You must mingle the tears with the joys and
    the blushes,—
  But it speeds like a train on the rail.—

Of the pictures of man that of age should be
    lightest,
  For the sun at his going away
Mostly smiles on the earth, it is then he is
    brightest,
  And with glory he closes the day.

Oh, grant to the mortals, that calmly surveying
  Old age with its winters of snow,
They may smile at the drifts while compla-
    cently staying,
  Nor tremble when summoned to go!

"THE SCENIC ROUTE."

If the people who travel alone for their pleasure,
Who have time at command and abundance of
    treasure,
Would but care less for fashion, and more for
    the learning,
There would be from old paths a distinctly
    marked turning.

Of the one who can stand where the Cæsars'
    bones moulder,
And not feel his blood now grow warmer
    now colder,
And whose thoughts will not wake by the
    Delphian fountain;
Be it said that his heart is like rock on the
    mountain.

By the graves of the great, where they silently
    slumber,
By the tombs of the bards of the undying
    number,
Oh, who would not stand, with his soul over-
    flowing
At the thoughts of the past, and the present
    fast going!

It is true that *our* land is not famed through
    the ages,

And far scattered the tombs of our bards and
    our sages;
When the eyes have beheld it, the heart
    proudly swelling
Must proclaim it *our* country, while glad tears
    are welling.

In the East old Niagara comes down with his
    thunders,
But I tell of the Rockies so rich in their
    wonders;
When you pass from the prairies like Eden
    appearing,
In a moment your train is mid mountains
    careering.

There, the Arkansas Cañon lies deep, dark
    appalling;
Where the sun never shines; with the bird ne-
    ver calling,
Save the bald eagle's cry, while exultingly
    soaring;
And no sound can be heard save the wild
    river's roaring.

Yes, the noise of the cars, and the engine's
    shrill clanging,
That are borne and re-echoed from cliffs over-
    hanging;
Supreme in their grandeur, majestic and
    towering

The mountains arise, all description o'erpower-
    ing.

Man forgets what he is, and his past recol-
    lection,
As surveying the scene he is lost in reflection;
While the Sangre de Cristo with snows ever-
    lasting,
When reflecting the sun, seems a vivid con-
    trasting.

By Mount Oury that stands lone and cold but
    eternal,
He will pass where the vales soon become sfot
    and vernal;
He will pass o'er the summit, and swiftly des-
    cending,
In the dells will be found a harmonious blend-
    ing.

On, on rolls his train, and he wakes from his
    sleeping,
While his mind must revert to the stage
    coaches' creeping;
He travels by palace, and he meets every
    season;
'T is a great panorama that staggers the
    reason.

No tongue has described it, no pen has por-
    trayed it,

All Nature seems proud that her hands have
    arrayed it;
She has clad it in sheen clear from ocean to
    ocean;
The land of our pride, and our fathers' de-
    votion.

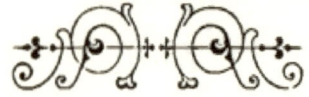

www.ingramcontent.com/pod-product-compliance
Lightning Source LLC
Chambersburg PA
CBHW032007010726
47493CB00007B/2305